How to Make a Wedding

Eloise Evans is an in-demand luxury bridal designer from Sydney.

Victoria Preston is a talented wedding cake creator from Boston.

Worlds apart, they should have only their industry in common, but they also share an unexpected bond—they're long-lost twin sisters!

Now, as their worlds collide, Eloise and Tori find the pieces of themselves they've always felt have been missing...just in time for each of them to find the love they deserve...

Read the twin sisters' stories in:

From Bridal Designer to Bride
By Kandy Shepherd

From Tropical Fling to Forever
By Nina Singh

Dear Reader,

This book was a special one for me to write. For one thing, it's book two of a duet with the incomparable author Kandy Shepherd. Her stories have always been some of my absolute favorites.

Kandy and I wanted to write about a set of young twin women who were separated at birth and only happened to find each other completely by chance decades after being adopted.

Tori Preston has always felt there was a figurative hole in her life, despite being part of a large and loving family. Finding her twin finally puts the missing puzzle piece firmly into place.

Fate also has another unexpected turn in store for her, however. Soon after discovering her sister, she's contracted to work as the on-site baker for a destination wedding in the Bahamas.

She's a professional on an assignment and needs to focus, but things quickly turn personal as the attraction between her and the bride's brother, Clay, is immediate and fierce.

But Clay and Tori's attraction soon proves impossible to ignore. They'll both have to overcome their past wounds in order to move on together.

I hope you enjoy their story.

Nina

From Tropical Fling to Forever

Nina Singh

Recycling programs
for this product may
not exist in your area.

ISBN-13: 978-1-335-56699-7

From Tropical Fling to Forever

Copyright © 2021 by Nilay Nina Singh

This edition published by arrangement with Harlequin Books S.A.

For questions and comments about the quality of this book, please contact us at CustomerService@Harlequin.com.

Harlequin Enterprises ULC
22 Adelaide St. West, 40th Floor
Toronto, Ontario M5H 4E3, Canada
www.Harlequin.com

Printed in U.S.A.

Nina Singh lives just outside Boston, Massachusetts, with her husband, children and a very rambunctious Yorkie. After several years in the corporate world, she finally followed the advice of family and friends to "give the writing a go, already." She's oh-so-happy she did. When not at her keyboard, she likes to spend time on the tennis court or golf course. Or immersed in a good read.

Books by Nina Singh

Harlequin Romance

Destination Brides

Swept Away by the Venetian Millionaire

The Men Who Make Christmas

Snowed in with the Reluctant Tycoon

9 to 5

Miss Prim and the Maverick Millionaire

The Marriage of Inconvenience
Reunited with Her Italian Billionaire
Tempted by Her Island Millionaire
Christmas with Her Secret Prince
Captivated by the Millionaire
Their Festive Island Escape
Her Billionaire Protector
Spanish Tycoon's Convenient Bride
Her Inconvenient Christmas Reunion

Visit the Author Profile page at Harlequin.com.

To my dear friends and colleagues in the writing community whom I didn't get to see in person this year. I miss you all.

Praise for
Nina Singh

"A captivating holiday adventure! *Their Festive Island Escape* by Nina Singh is a twist on an enemies-to-lovers trope and is sure to delight. I recommend this book to anyone.... It's fun, it's touching and it's satisfying."

—*Goodreads*

CHAPTER ONE

PERHAPS THE TWO-INCH heels might have been a bit much.

Victoria Preston stepped into the kitchen of the corner bakery she owned and operated. Removing an apron from the wall hook, she started to put it on, hoping her atypical attire didn't draw attention. No such luck. The other woman in the room immediately stopped what she was doing and took a good look.

"Wow, aren't you looking sharp! What's the occasion, Tori?"

Yep. She should have worn sensible sandals. No doubt she'd be having that very thought later again today after closing, when her feet were sore and achy.

Tori didn't quite meet her baker assistant's eyes as she answered. "No occasion. Just wanted to dress up a little today, that's all."

Shawna quirked an eyebrow and studied Tori from the rose-pink-painted nails in her open-toed heels to the loose bun atop her head. "Right."

Luckily, Shawna dropped the subject as she lifted a heavy bag of flour and poured what she needed into an industrial-size silver mixing bowl.

Not that Tori could blame the woman for noticing. Truth was, before discovering and reuniting with her long-lost, estranged twin sister not that long ago, Tori would have pegged herself as the last woman on earth to dress up for the sake of a man. She'd always preferred being less visible, didn't like to call attention to herself. But discovering the existence of her twin had led to Tori's reexamination of her life. Part of that scrutiny had included an undertaking to be bolder, more daring. Nothing like discovering an identical twin to make you contemplate your life's choices.

"Thanks for covering the early shift," Tori said to her most loyal employee, who also happened to be her dearest and most trusted friend since high school.

"You know I prefer it."

"And thank heavens for that." Tori was full of gratitude. She'd never been a morning person—definitely more of a night owl. Not a good trait for a bakery owner. It was the one aspect of her career choice she didn't love. Everything else about it, she absolutely adored. The creativity, the delicious aromas constantly surrounding her, the freedom to do her own thing. The excitement of not knowing who was going to walk through the front door from day to day yet also having regular customers she considered friends after these past three years.

"The muffins are in the oven, the bread is in the warmer and the scones are cooling on racks," Shawna informed her.

"You're too good to me. Gives me a chance to double-check inventory and figure out exactly what we need. There's a specialty order coming in later today." Her heart flipped in her chest as she thought of the customer placing that order. So foolish of her. The man probably didn't give her so much as a passing thought until he needed baked goods. While scarcely a day went by where she didn't think of him.

He'd called last night to announce he'd be arriving sometime after the lunch rush. He'd said no more than that.

Clayton Ramos. Most of the world referred to him as Clay.

How embarrassing that she'd felt the need to dress up just because he was coming. As if she wouldn't be covered in flour and chocolate syrup by midmorning anyway.

"What kind of specialty order?" Shawna

asked, gazing at her intently. "The tall, dark and handsome kind?"

"I don't know what you could possibly mean."

Shawna laughed. "I mean that you don't typically dress up for a Tuesday spent baking and waiting on customers. Want to tell me about it?"

Her friend was far too observant. Tori should have known she wouldn't let the subject drop for long.

Tori put her hands on her hips. "If you must know, I'm meeting with a rather important client later." She motioned to the dress beneath her apron. "And it's hardly a ball gown."

"Which important client?" Shawna wanted to know, ignoring the latter comment.

Tori tried to feign indifference when she answered. "Mr. Ramos called last night to say he wanted to stop by to discuss an order."

"Oh really?"

"Yes."

"Funny, isn't it?" Shawna quipped, a mischievous hitch in her tone.

"What?"

"How Mr. Ramos's visit just happens to coincide with the same day you happen to run out of clean laundry and have to wear a silk wrap dress to work."

Tori didn't bother to suppress her chuckle. She should have known better than to try to pull the wool over her best friend's eyes. Time to come clean.

She leaned her hip against the counter and faced her assistant. "Okay. Fine. I wanted to look my best for one of our more…exclusive clients. Is that so wrong?"

Shawna gave her a wink. "Now, was that so hard to admit? To your best friend?"

Sometimes Tori wished said best friend didn't know her quite so well. "Now, don't go reading into things. I just wanted to look a bit more professional. That's all."

"Sure." Shawna shrugged dismissively. "Let's go with that."

Tori ignored the gibe and began preparing the counter with an eye toward the clock. The hour before opening the bakery doors always seemed to move at lightning speed. Today was no exception.

"When is he due in?" Shawna asked.

"He wasn't very specific. Just said sometime in the afternoon, after the lunch rush."

"I wonder what he has in mind."

Tori had been speculating that question all night. Only one conclusion came to mind that made the most sense. "Maybe another wedding he needs a cake for. He does have another younger sister."

Shawna yelped an excited squeal. "Then that would make us one of the first few to know about a potential wedding. Like the last time."

"And we will be absolutely discreet. Like the last time," Tori echoed.

It had taken a good two months for the attention of various paparazzi and news outlets to settle down once the world had learned her bakery would be the pastry and cake provider for a wedding thrown by the one and only Clayton Ramos. Clayton was a celebrated architect to the stars and a globally sought-after bachelor.

The publicity had been great for business, of course. But the attention had often been nerve-racking, draining. Still, the attention had put Tori's Pastries on the map in a way that would be hard to duplicate.

Unlike Tori, Shawna had reveled in the spotlight, enjoyed every bit of the attention. She'd even gone out with a couple of the photographers and a blogger who'd showcased the bakery. No doubt she was excited at the prospect of it all happening again. Her next words confirmed it. "I wonder if the local news will want to run a spot on us this time, too. It's all so exciting."

Indeed. Tori had a feeling Clay's reappearance in her life would cause as much chaos and disruption as the last time.

One more disruption and Clay figured his focus would be completely shot for the day.

He really should call the bakery to reschedule. But he found he really didn't want to. For reasons he couldn't quite explain, he'd been looking forward to stopping in. It absolutely had nothing to do with the perky, cheerful owner with the sparkling green eyes and cute pert nose. No, that wasn't it at all.

Ha. He knew he was fooling himself. In truth, he was looking forward to seeing her—which made no sense whatsoever. He didn't even know her, despite the fact she'd made a handful of desserts and cakes for him over the past couple of years.

"Are you even listening, Clay?" his sister's voice demanded through the speaker of his cell phone. He hadn't even noticed she'd stopped talking.

Clay pinched the bridge of his nose. He'd obviously missed something in the conversation. Right on cue, the dramatics kicked in.

Gemma had always been the more theatrical of his two sisters. She was especially on edge now that she was due to be married in a few weeks.

Clay had been the only father figure his younger sisters had had since the three of them had barely said goodbye to their single-digit ages. Now, even as adults, the girls turned to him for solutions whenever anything went awry in their lives. He'd vowed long ago to always be there for them. And, so far, he'd managed to keep that vow. But heaven knew, it could all be so draining.

"Of course, I am," he answered.

"Do you think she'll say yes?" Gemma asked. "I really prefer her to anyone else. It is a big ask. It's not like we're simply asking her for a cake this time."

"I'm counting on it," he reassured her. After all, if the pretty baker didn't agree at first, he would simply negotiate until she did.

By the time he ended the call with his sister, he'd accepted that he was far too distracted to get any more work done in the office.

Though it was much too early for their scheduled meeting, he could use a strong cup of coffee like the brew served at the bakery. And a fresh, hot croissant would certainly hit the spot.

Why not? Decision made, Clay packed up his laptop and gathered his design tools. As he locked up behind him, he thought about his sister's question. Gemma was right. It was a fairly big ask that he was about to present to Ms. Victoria Preston. But he'd gotten pretty far in life by determining what he wanted and then doing whatever it took to go about getting it. He needed her services. He would get them.

He was about to make one Boston North End bakery owner an offer she couldn't refuse.

When her cell phone vibrated in her apron pocket, Tori didn't even have to look at the screen to know who was calling. Her intuition told her. Eloise termed it "twin sense." It still somewhat amazed Tori that up until a short while ago, she hadn't even known about the existence of her twin sister. Now, Eloise was an integral part of her entire being. Even when she traveled thousands of miles away to her home city of Sydney, Australia.

Pulling out the chair of the table she'd been wiping down in the dining area, she answered the video call.

Discovering Eloise's existence had been the shock of her life, but a part of Tori had always known. A part of her psyche had always reached out for something or someone, had known it was there for her to grasp.

"Hey, sis!" Eloise's smiling face greeted her from the small screen.

A surge of happiness flooded through Tori. Her twin never failed to lift her spirits. "Hey back."

"He'll be there later today then?" Eloise asked.

Tori used the phone grip on the back of her cell to prop it on the table.

"Why, whatever are you referring to?" She barely got the words out before she had to stifle a small giggle. She'd told Eloise about Clay's impending visit last night...when she'd called her sister right after hanging up with him.

Eloise wagged a finger. "Don't pretend you don't know what I'm talking about."

Tori had to laugh. "Okay. Sorry. Won't happen again."

"I would hope not. When is he due in?"

Tori glanced at the time above the screen. "In a few hours."

"You ready for him?"

Her heart leaped in her chest at the wording of her question. Maybe she'd divulged a bit too much about her feelings when she'd confided in her sister about him. "It's just a business meeting, Eloise. That's all."

"Doesn't have to be. I did some digging and looked him up after what you told me last night. That man is the straight-up definition of 'stone-melting hot.' I say you make a move."

Tori rolled her eyes. "You know me better than that, Eloise." How true. Her twin knew her better than anyone else on earth did—despite not having set eyes on each other until just a few weeks ago.

"She has your same exact face," an all too familiar voice said from over her shoulder. *His* voice. Tori didn't have to turn around to confirm that Clayton Ramos was standing right behind her.

Tori jumped out of her chair in shock, fire rushing to her cheeks in sheer embarrassment. Heavens, what if he'd heard? How utterly mortifying.

To her further horror, her leap had sent the chair careening backward. Tori reached out to try to catch it in a desperate attempt to keep it from crashing at his feet. Only, he did the same at the same time. The collision was unavoidable. As was the ensuing disaster that unfolded when Clay lost his grip on his extralarge cup of iced coffee, black. The cap flew off and the contents splashed like an upended bucket across his face and the front of his shirt.

From Tori's cell phone, Eloise's stunned voice echoed through the air. "Oh, Tori. Oh no."

Despite the words, Tori's "twin sense"

told her that her sister was more than a little amused.

She quickly said goodbye and pocketed her phone.

Every eye in the bakery was on them, laser-focused on the bizarre scene that had just unfolded. Tori just wanted to disappear into thin air. For his part, Clay looked a bit shell-shocked as he studied the ever-growing splotch of dark brown spreading across his crisp white shirt.

You can dress a girl up...

"I'm so sorry!" Reaching for a handful of napkins from the dispenser on the table behind her, Tori tried to repair some of the damage, but all she managed was to further spread the blasted stain.

Shawna chose that moment to come out from the back. Taking in the disastrous scene, she clutched her hand to her chest. "Oh my, what happened?" Her voice shook ever so slightly.

Tori glanced over her shoulder to see her friend's lips quivering. Yep, she was definitely trying not to chuckle. How wonderful that Tori could be such a source of humor for two of the most important women in her life.

"I'll get a towel," Shawna declared, disappearing behind the swinging doors.

"Mr. Ramos, I'm so incredibly sorry," Tori

repeated for the third time as she grabbed more napkins and continued the useless dabbing. "It's just, I didn't hear you approach from behind me, and our appointment isn't until much later. I didn't see you come in at all." Now she was just rambling.

He wrapped long fingers gently around her wrist. "Please stop. It's clearly not working."

He was certainly right about that. To make matters worse, there was the clear sound of snickering from more than one patron. Tori wanted to cry. Of all the ways she'd imagined their scheduled meeting would go, thoroughly humiliating herself had not been one of them.

"I'm so terr—"

He cut her off with an upheld palm. "Please. Don't apologize again."

She had to bite down on her lip to follow his direction.

"Besides," he added, "it was clearly my fault."

It was?

"I shouldn't have startled you. I'm the one who should be apologizing."

That was ridiculous. Only one of them was wearing a drenched and soggy shirt, for heaven's sake. The person with black iced coffee dripping down his shirtfront should most definitely not be the one to apologize. Still, Tori was at a loss for words. For him to try to take responsibility for something that was so clearly her doing, floored her.

Aside from her father and brothers, she hadn't really come across too many men who would do such a thing.

Shawna returned with a terry towel and tossed it to Tori. She held it out to him, but Clay didn't bother taking it. He just gave her a nod. What was the use? He was right; any attempt to blot the liquid was beyond pointless.

"So much for getting some work done." He cursed under his breath, adding some other muttered words she couldn't quite make out. Words that might have included "day from hell."

"I beg your pardon?" she asked.

"Nothing. I've just been having a bit of a vexing one."

"I'm so—" He cut her a sharp look and she stopped herself from apologizing yet again.

"Guess I have no choice but to head home and change. I'll come back for our meeting at the hour we scheduled. Not that I can spare the time today of all days."

"Don't leave."

He blinked at her then glanced down his chest. "Well, I can hardly sit here soaked to the skin." He leaned closer to her, as if to share a secret. "It's rather uncomfortable."

"I live in the apartment upstairs. I'll get you a shirt you can wear."

He studied her from head to toe and she felt a warmth creep into her cheeks. "Uh, thanks for the offer, but I'm guessing we're not the same size."

"Not my shirt."

His eyebrow shot up. "I don't think your boyfriend would appreciate—"

This time she cut him off. "Oh no! It's not like that."

"It isn't?"

Why had she suddenly lost the ability to communicate? The last thing Tori wanted was for Clay to think she was romantically attached to someone. And that was quite the acknowledgment, now that she thought about it.

Giving her head a shake, she tried to get her tongue to work properly. "I have two older brothers." Three, if she counted Josh. "I've confiscated more than my share of large T-shirts to sleep in."

Something flittered behind his eyes before he responded. "I see."

"Plus, I'm due to do a load of laundry. I'll just throw your shirt in, too, before any staining sets in. It will be washed and dry for you in a couple of hours."

"Huh." He seemed to consider it then nodded. "In that case, I think I will take you up on the offer."

Tori turned on her heel to head upstairs and retrieve the shirt. To her surprise, Clay followed her.

She'd fully intended to run down with a T-shirt and wait for him to change in the restroom so she could run back up to launder his shirt. But he clearly intended to follow her.

Of course, that made more sense—for him to just change in her apartment. So why was her pulse quickening at the thought of him being up there? She would look foolish and possibly offend him if she asked him not to follow her.

Had she even bothered to put away the breakfast dishes this morning? Or last night's dinner dishes, for that matter? Probably not. It had been a long, busy, and exhausting day at the bakery yesterday and she'd barely had the energy to kick her shoes off and scarf down a cheese croissant with a small salad. Though, in her defense, she hadn't been expecting *the* Clayton Ramos to be paying her a house visit.

Oh dear. What if he thought her a slob after seeing the state of her apartment? What if she'd never picked up the shoes she'd kicked off after arriving home? Or discarded the left-over ice cream carton? What if—?

She cut off the thought. Those days of being judged by a man were well past now. And she had no intention of going back to them.

"I appreciate this," Clay was saying behind her. "I'm already delayed on this next design, and phase two of the project is fast approaching."

"It's the least I can do. I feel terrible about what happened."

"Hey, don't worry about it, okay? It's not the first time I've had a drink spilled on me."

She stifled a chuckle. "Happens often, does it?"

"Let's just say that the last time someone threw an icy drink in my direction, I most determinedly deserved it."

Tori glanced back to find him flashing her a devilish grin that had her faltering a step.

By the time they walked through the storage room and up the back stairs to the front door of her second-floor apartment, Tori had somewhat convinced herself to calm down. Turning the unlocked knob, she stepped aside to let him enter ahead of her.

The calm faded as Clay immediately started to shrug out of his shirt.

He was clearly comfortable disrobing in ladies' apartments. Not surprising, based on his reputation as an international player. Who was the latest girlfriend rumored to be again? Oh yeah, the Austrian model. He'd been snapped walking out of her apartment building in the wee hours of the morning just last month.

Clay handed her the shirt and, for a moment, she couldn't move as she took it from his hand.

She was staring. Tori forced herself to look away. Not that it was easy. Sweet cupcakes, it was hard not to stare at him standing there in front of her all bare-chested. Golden-tanned. Chisel-muscled.

Stop it.

This was so not the time to be thinking along those lines.

"I'll get you that T-shirt," she managed to utter, hoping beyond hope she'd turned away before he'd noticed her ever-reddening cheeks.

Something told her it was wishful thinking.

How in the world had he ended up here?

Clay stood in the middle of the room, taking in his surroundings. Soft and rounded. Those two words described the space perfectly. A plush sofa sat in the center, atop an oval area rug that appeared to be hand woven. A large round mirror hung above an arched fireplace mantel. No sharp angles. His trained eye told him the circular theme had been deliberate. The occupant knew what she was doing when decorating this living space. These choices had been thought out and planned on a specific preference.

Victoria Preston did not like sharp edges.

He could hear her scrummaging around somewhere down the hallway. If someone had told him this morning that later that day he'd be waiting in Ms. Preston's charming apartment while shirtless and smelling of strong espresso…well, he wasn't sure what he would have thought.

But perhaps a better question was how had he forgotten her pretty eyes. Or the contrast the color of those eyes made with her spiky auburn hair…

Steady there, fella.

He really didn't need his thoughts to head in that direction. Tori, as everyone seemed to call her, was so not his usual type. She was too sweet, too unassuming. A woman like that didn't need the likes of him marring their well-planned, idyllic lives.

That's why it had made no sense earlier, the hollow feeling in his gut when he'd thought she'd be giving him a shirt that belonged to a boyfriend. Or the sense of relief he'd experienced once she'd corrected his assumption. For all he knew, she may very well have a significant other. Just one who didn't own apparel she found adequate as sleepwear. Women like Tori weren't often single. Not for long, anyway. Successful, smart, attractive—she could have her pick of men.

Really, it was none of his business at all.

He studied her apartment a little closer. It suited her. Tidy overall, aside from a couple of used dishes on the kitchen counter behind the living area. Not a speck of dust to be seen. Exactly the type of apartment he would have picked for her. Framed photographs littered almost every surface. Pictures filled with smiling faces against backdrops of scenic landscapes or charming rooms.

A raggedy, frayed and torn stuffed rabbit hugged a corner of the cream-colored couch. The thing had to be ancient.

Her place was cozy. Comfortable. Judging by the photos of her throughout the years, he could tell she'd live the kind of childhood he and his sisters had never experienced growing up.

A more recent photograph sitting on the circular marble coffee table in the center of the room caught his eye. Tori with another young woman who looked exactly like her. Only the hair was different. Whereas Tori wore hers short and spiky in an unconventional, rather modern style—he believed the kids would call it Goth—the other woman had wavier locks, a shade different.

She had a twin.

That explained what he'd seen on her phone screen earlier, what had led to the chain of events that had ultimately had him smelling like a coffee grinder.

Funny. He'd hired her more than once over the past three years—and they'd made plenty of small talk—but he didn't recall her ever mentioning a sister, much less a twin. Or maybe she had and he just hadn't been listening. How often in his life had he been told he was too distracted?

Always got your head in the clouds...always thinking you're better than everyone else.

Tori walked back into the room at that moment, dispelling the cruel memory. One of all too many.

She handed him a soft cotton T-shirt. Gray with bold blue FDNY letters across the front.

"Thanks. I take it one of your brothers is a fireman? In New York City?"

"An EMT."

"Ah." He took the shirt and pulled it over his head. A little snug, but it fit well enough.

It smelled of Tori, a blend of berries and citrus and something appealingly spicy. Cinnamon maybe. Or cloves.

"Your shirt is already in the washer," she told him.

"Thanks." He pointed to the framed photo he'd been staring at when she'd walked in. "You never mentioned a sister."

She inhaled deeply. "That's because I didn't really know until recently that…" She looked down at her toes, grasping for words, it seemed. "It's actually a really long story, and I should probably get back downstairs. Shawna is by herself with cakes in the oven and customers waiting. We're a bit short-staffed until the afternoon."

"Of course," he responded immediately. "I didn't mean to hold you up. Or to pry." He felt compelled to add that last part because of the underlying tension in her tone.

"Oh, no. It's not that." She smiled and her whole face transformed, a brightness appearing behind her eyes. "I actually would like to tell you about it sometime. It's kind of a crazy tale."

"Then I'll look forward to hearing it. Consider me intrigued."

It surprised him just how much he meant that.

CHAPTER TWO

TORI FELT AN almost silly rush of relief once Clay put the T-shirt on. The man simply looked much too good topless. She gave herself a mental forehead thwack for acting like a schoolgirl with her first crush.

But was there really any harm in that? This was just some simple and innocent fantasizing on her part. Clay was ridiculously out of her league. He dated actresses and dancers, for heaven's sake. Plus, she presently had no desire or inclination to pursue any kind of romantic relationship. Not after she'd tried so hard to move on after her last one. Her only one.

She was finally at a point where she wasn't constantly looking over her shoulder or bracing herself for the next put-down.

Tori was perfectly content to live the single, unattached life for the moment. In fact, she'd never felt more at peace in years, not since that first date with Drew at the naïve and fresh age of seventeen.

Though it was hard to imagine turning a man like Clay down—if by some miracle he were even to ask her out.

And that was about as likely as bread rising without yeast.

Clay cleared his throat and she realized she'd drifted off into her own thoughts.

"I'll get your shirt back to you as soon as it's dry," she said and turned toward the door.

To her surprise, he stopped her with a hand on her forearm. The casual touch sent a tingle of electricity straight through to her chest. "If we could just have another minute…"

She blinked up at him.

"Since we happen to be here alone, I thought we could just discuss the matter I came here to see you about," he added.

Tori had to swallow the breath that had lodged in her throat. "Y-yes?"

"We were quite pleased with the cake you created for my sister Adria's wedding a couple of years back."

"Thank you."

"My other sister, Gemma, will also be getting married in a few weeks."

"I see. You want to discuss contracting for another cake then?"

"In a sense."

What in the world did that mean? And why would he want to have the conversation here in her apartment?

"Um, what dates were you thinking? And how many tiers?"

"The truth is, I don't really know," he said. "Gemma will have to tell you herself."

Clearly, Tori was missing something since it appeared his sister wouldn't even be joining them for the conversation. "I don't understand. You are here to hire me to make a cake, correct?"

"Sort of."

An uneasy feeling began to rise in her chest. Maybe he didn't want her at all for this gig. Maybe he was simply too nice and wanted to tell her she was being replaced face-to-face. "Sort of?"

"I wanted to meet with you because I'd like to speak to you about a job offer."

Tori blinked, trying to process the information. It didn't make any sense, so she stated the obvious. "I own my own business. I don't really need a job."

Clay pinched the bridge of his nose. "I'm sorry. I'm not really explaining this well. Maybe it would be clearer if I referred to it as a business opportunity."

Nope. Not clearer at all. No matter what he called it, she couldn't make sense of what was going on here.

"I think you might want to just come out and tell me exactly what this is all about, Clay."

"Right." He clasped his hands in front of him. "I'll preface it by saying I know how busy you are, how in demand your services are... So I know this might be asking a lot."

"Okay."

"My sister is having a destination wedding," he explained. "It's to take place over the span of five days on a small Bahamian island resort off the coast of Florida."

That made no sense. How was Tori supposed to get a cake delivered across land and sea to some island in the Bahamas? "And...?"

"And I'd like you to come along."

Tori gave her head a shake, as if to clear it. Had she heard him correctly? "Are you...asking me to your sister's wedding?"

As soon as the words left her mouth, Tori wanted to somehow suck them back in. Then she wanted to sink through the floor at the look of utter horror on Clay's face. She wouldn't forget that look for as long as she lived.

How breathtakingly humiliating. She'd gone and made the most embarrassing of assumptions: that he might actually be asking her to attend his sister's wedding as some kind of date.

Clearly, he'd had something else in mind.

"Gemma would like to bring along both a meal chef and a pastry chef to work the wedding," he quickly began to explain. "The latter being you."

Her mouth had gone dry but somehow Tori managed to answer. "I see."

"Gemma, my sister who's getting married," he added, abruptly blurting it out as if that fact hadn't already been made abundantly clear.

What a fool she was to even consider for a moment that he would ask her for anything even remotely personal.

Lifting her chin, Tori gave him the only answer she could if she had any hope of saving face. "I'm sorry, Clay. Thank you for the offer. But I'm afraid I can't take you up on it."

CHAPTER THREE

Three weeks later

WHAT IN THE world had she been thinking?

Tori adjusted her roomy bucket seat, tilted it slightly back and then turned to a fresh sheet on her sketch pad. She'd never been on a private jet before.

Clayton Ramos certainly knew how to drive a hard bargain. She had to give him that.

Who would have thought, after that afternoon in her apartment when Clay had made his offer, that she'd be southbound above the Atlantic on his private aircraft less than a month later? She'd resisted in the beginning. She really had. But he'd continually sweetened the deal to the point she'd have been a fool to turn it down. In the end, Tori had done what was best for the bakery. On top of the monetary incentive, she couldn't deny what the opportunity would do for her small shop. Tori's

Pastries was managing quite well, if she did say so herself, but customers could be fickle.

Look at what had happened to her sister. A disgruntled and overly demanding influencer had almost destroyed Eloise's career as well as her reputation. Luckily, Josh and her sister had devised a rather unconventional plan to thwart the woman's cruel intentions. They'd had to go through the ruse of a relationship, but given it had led to a real wedding, everything had all worked out in the end.

The memory brought a smile to Tori's face.

But, fake relationship aside, the threat to Eloise's bridal dress design business had been much too real.

All it would take for something similar to happen to Tori would be one too many bad online reviews. She spent a fair amount of time monitoring such reviews. Luckily, most of what was written about her bakery was positive. But there were always the select few who found ways to criticize. The cupcakes were too sweet. The lines on weekends were too long. One customer had had the nerve to write that her red velvet cupcakes tasted like store-bought mix. It was her top-selling item, for heaven's sake!

Forgetting her sketch pad for the moment, Tori sighed softly to herself as she looked out the window. The rest of the wedding party had flown to Nassau earlier in the week and everyone was now waiting for Tori and Clay to arrive. Once they did, the group would all sail to the small island where the ceremony was to take place.

Clay, having had to stay behind for an important meeting, had suggested Tori travel with him since she hadn't been able to make the earlier flight.

Despite the size of the impressive plane, there was something quite intimate about being alone with Clay hundreds of feet up in the air. She glanced at him now.

As if sensing her gaze, he looked up and caught her eye. Tori resisted the urge to look away. It was much too late to pretend she hadn't been studying him.

He slowly shut his laptop and pushed back the tray table. Standing, he made his way toward her.

Taking the seat across from hers, he pointed to the graphic tee she was wearing. Imprinted with an image of a bowl of spaghetti, the italic lettering underneath read Vilardo's.

"That place isn't too far from your bakery. I've eaten there. Excellent restaurant."

She could only agree. "I like it a lot, too."

"It can be impossible to get a table some days."

"I've seen the line snake around the corner at times."

He nodded. "Worth the wait, though. The food is incomparable."

"It's often written up as one of the top five trattorias in Boston's North End."

He shook his head. "I'd say top three. The stuffed pasta shells are a work of art."

"I'll be sure to tell my mama you think so," she told him with a smile of pride.

"Your mama?"

"It's my parents' restaurant. My mother's maiden name is Vilardo."

Clay's eyes narrowed on her face. "Huh. Guess the food business runs in the blood."

This was the awkward part. Tori never knew how to respond to such comments. She usually brushed off the words with a polite smile or a deft change of subject. But this time felt different. For reasons she couldn't really articulate, she wanted Clay to know about this large part of her story. She even wanted to tell him about the utterly unbelievable way she'd found her sister. She had no idea why, but she found him easy to confide in. That was almost silly. She barely knew the man.

"Blood wouldn't really apply in my case," she told him.

He lifted an eyebrow in puzzlement. "Oh?"

"I was adopted as a toddler."

"Family doesn't always mean blood." He sounded like he was speaking from experience.

"Nurture versus nature, I suppose."

"Either way, your parents must be very proud of you."

Tori turned to look out the small window again. Outside, myriad thick, bouncy clouds littered the light blue sky. If only she could emphatically nod her head and agree with Clay's last statement. But she'd be lying. While it was true her parents were indeed very proud of her in many ways, they were also severely disappointed.

And there was no way she would be able to make them understand. Not without revealing a truth that would crush their spirits.

From where he stood, Tori wasn't looking all that great. Clay dropped the design specs he'd been reviewing and made his way over to where she sat portside. He couldn't seem to stay away from the woman; she pulled him like no one else he'd ever met.

"You're not getting seasick, are you?" he asked, sitting in the booth across from hers.

They'd landed at Nassau's Lynden Pindling International Airport about two hours ago. After clearing customs and meeting up with the rest of the wedding party, they'd immediately boarded a passenger catamaran to sail to their final destination.

Studying Tori now, he had no doubt her pallor was off.

"Maybe a little," she answered in a small voice. "Which makes no sense. I've been on plenty of boats on choppy Cape Cod waters."

"Though not after a long plane ride, I'm guessing."

She scoffed with a smile, looking out over the water. "A plane ride on a private jet is hardly something to complain about."

He shrugged. "It still makes for a long day of travel. And there was quite a bit of turbulence."

"Thanks for trying to make me feel like less of a wimp."

Wimp. Not a word he would ever use to describe her. Anyone who had opened their own business in a severely competitive field and was running it successfully almost entirely on her own was the antithesis of a wimp. "There're a couple of doctors and NPs among the guests on board. Would you like me to ask around to see if anyone might have something to help?"

Tori shook her head, the motion making her skin shade even greener. Even so, she still looked mind-scramblingly attractive. Funny. And why would his thoughts be going in that direction at such an inopportune time?

"I'll be fine," she said, turning her eyes toward the water once more. "I just need to sit here and focus on the horizon. That's supposed to help with mild motion sickness, isn't it?"

"I'll go get you a soda." He stood before she could protest and retrieved a ginger ale from the stocked bar set up for them.

He popped open the can and set it on the table in front of her.

"Thanks. Sorry to be a bother."

"You're hardly a bother, Tori. And I can't tell you how much I appreciate you coming along to do this for Gemma." He motioned to where his sister stood leaning against her groom. His other sister, Adria, was huddled with her young daughter over a tablet, watching a fairy-tale movie they'd downloaded before the trip.

"You and your siblings seem very close," Tori said, taking a small sip from the can.

"We're pretty much all we have."

She looked at him in question but he had no desire to get into the wreck that was his family history. "What about you?" he asked, changing the subject. "You have two older brothers, correct? Are you close with them?"

The truth was she adored them both. "They do their fair share of brotherly teasing. But yes, I would say we are close." Her gaze shifted back to the horizon. "I'm close with my sister, as well. We are twins, after all."

"That's right. She's the woman I saw on your phone screen that day." Tori'd spoken often of her brothers during their past interactions, but finding out she'd had a twin had come as a bit of a surprise to him. It was all very peculiar.

"Did you two play any twin pranks growing up? Switch spots in class to try to confuse people?"

Her smile faltered. "We didn't actually grow up together."

Peculiar indeed. She solved the mystery with her next words. "I mentioned that I was adopted as a toddler. As was she, but to a different family. I've been told it was a private adoption necessitated when my biological mother became ill. The agency decided it was best if we completely cut all ties and contact. Eloise and I had no say in the matter."

"Interesting," was all he could come up with to say. It appeared he wasn't the only one with an unconventional family dynamic.

"I found her completely by accident. Well, my friend Josh did, to be more accurate." An affectionate smile bloomed on her lips. "I've known him for as long as I can remember."

Clay's chest constricted at the way her face brightened when she'd mentioned the man's name. "Your friend Josh found your long-lost sister?"

She nodded, her smile widening. "He's something else. A true one in a million."

Quite the accolade, Clay thought. Who exactly was this guy? Every indication, from her expression to her tone of voice, hinted that he was much more than a friend.

Clay had no reason to want to question her about him, to find out exactly who this man was to her. Still, the tightening in his chest had yet to ease. Until he heard her next words.

"Eloise and Josh are married now. I was a bridesmaid."

A surge of relief Clay couldn't really explain flushed through him at the revelation. Tori and Josh were clearly no more than lifelong friends who now found themselves in-laws. Not that it was any of his business. The woman was simply here to bake, for goodness' sake. He shouldn't be interested in her life relationships.

Still, he couldn't help but feel moved by what she'd just told him. The discovery of a long-lost sibling as an adult wasn't a tale one heard every day.

"I've shocked you," Tori said with a smile after several moments of silence. She appeared to be feeling better. Some of the color had begun to appear on her cheeks and her lips weren't drawn quite so rigidly any longer.

"It's quite a story. I'm glad you and your sister found each other."

"Our connection was immediate. Now, it's like we were never apart. She's in the process of moving to Boston and opening another store."

There was no mistaking the pride in Tori's voice.

"What does she do?"

"She designs bridal dresses. For a very high-end clientele."

"Seems that's yet another connection. You do wedding cakes, she designs wedding dresses."

Tori ducked her head. "Not quite the same. I'm simply a baker. And you happen to be my only high-end client."

Clay was struck by the defeatism of her words. For such an accomplished woman, she seemed to have a warped sense of personal achievement at such a young age. "I get the feeling I'll be one of many. And I doubt it will take long."

Her eyes grew wide at the compliment. He'd clearly surprised her.

"Thank you for saying that." She lifted the now empty soda can. "And thank you for this. Seems to have done the trick."

"You're welcome. Glad to hear it."

He was also glad to have learned a bit more about the woman he was finding more and more fascinating with each passing moment.

"Do you play tennis?"

Shading her eyes from the sun, Tori looked up from her lounge chair where she'd been relaxing on the beach and sketching for the better part of an hour. It was their second day on the island and so far she'd baked a cupcake tower to follow this evening's dinner and was now stealing some time to work on the design of the wedding cake. So focused on the task, she hadn't noticed the shadow that fell over the paper until she heard the all too familiar voice.

"Sorry to interrupt," Clay said, pointing to her sketch. "But it's something of an emergency."

The slight tilt at the corners of his mouth told her the emergency couldn't be all that pressing.

"Beg your pardon?"

"I asked if you played. Tennis."

She thought she'd heard the rather random question correctly. "I went to a summer camp every year until I turned thirteen. Tennis was part of the curriculum."

"Excellent." He reached for her hand. "I'll come with you as you get your sneakers."

Tori let him take her hand in his and slowly rose out of the chair. "I'm not quite sure I understand still."

"My sister and her groom have challenged me to a doubles match with a partner of my choice," he told her.

That didn't exactly explain why she was the choice in question. "And you're asking me?"

"Yes. And you're agreeing. Unless you really don't want to."

Tori was still processing what was happening. He took advantage of her hesitation. "Come on. It'll do you good to get some air and exercise. And you can help me beat those two. They've been talking smack all morning."

Everyone else must have turned him down. Why else would he be dragging the pastry chef along to play as his partner?

"But I didn't bring a racket or anything."

He shrugged. "The resort provides those."

"Was there no one else?"

He stopped walking and turned to her. "I'm

starting to get the feeling you're not very enthusiastic to play with me."

The utter ridiculousness of the situation and the deadpan seriousness in his voice had Tori struggling to suppress a laugh. "It's not that. I'm just curious as to why you're asking the pastry chef when you have guests you can ask."

"I suppose I can go around the resort looking for someone. But it's going to get too hot to play in a bit. And here you are, right on the beach, sketching. Plus, you said you know how to play. It has to be fate, I'd say. Kismet even."

Well, when he put it that way. "I suppose that makes sense." Though she didn't quite know about the whole "fate" bit.

"Also, I'd like to play with you," he added with a devilish wink that had her knees growing weak.

"I guess it'd be nice to handle a racket again."

He didn't waste time waiting for a direct confirmation. "Let's go then."

In less than fifteen minutes, Tori, having changed into a shorts set and tennis shoes, found herself covering the deuce side.

Surprisingly, she and Clay appeared to make a good team. He seemed in tune with her play strategy and they did a good job with silent communication—understanding each other's hand gestures and unspoken plays. In no time, they had taken the lead and were able to maintain it for the match. Tori even managed to ace the groom, leading to the stroke that essentially won the set.

Before she knew what he was up to, Clay rushed over and lifted her up in the air, his arms tight around her middle. He swung her around with a resounding cheer.

Tori's pulse was pounding by the time he put her back on the ground. It was nothing more than a victory hug. But she couldn't deny the physical longing that had rushed through her when she'd found herself in Clay's arms.

Gemma and Tom approached from the other side of the net and Clay turned in their direction. If he was affected at all by their embrace, he certainly didn't show it. That only confirmed what she already knew. She had to fight her attraction to this man, for self-preservation.

"All right, big bro," Gemma said as the four of them shook hands. "You two won fair and square. A deal is a deal. Drinks are on us. See you in the tavern in twenty?"

"Ha, ha. That's really funny considering it's an all-inclusive resort."

Gemma stuck her tongue out at him. "Yes, but I'll still pay dearly by having to listen to you brag about your win. Probably incessantly, until the end of time."

Clay chuckled. "There is that."

Bride and groom clasped hands as they walked away. "See you later, Tori," Gemma called over her shoulder. "Nice game."

Tori couldn't help but stare after them. They seemed so happy, so in love. She thought she'd had that once, but her relationship with Drew had only seemed ideal from the outside. That's why it had been so hard to explain to her family why she'd ultimately walked away. As much as she could explain, that is. She hadn't been able to bring herself to tell them the full extent of what had happened between her and her ex-boyfriend.

Her pride wouldn't allow it.

As a result, her friends and family all thought she was foolish for leaving a man that so many women would feel beyond fortunate to be with. Especially someone like her.

"Did you want to freshen up before heading over to the tavern?" Clay asked as they exited the court gates, pulling her out of her thoughts.

She knew should say no; turn him down flat. She was essentially his employee and fraternizing with the boss probably wasn't a good idea. "I should get back to sketching out the cake."

"Come on," he urged. "I can hardly take a victory lap without my play partner."

Tori faltered. One drink wouldn't hurt, would it? She really was rather thirsty after close to ninety minutes of hard play in the strong sun. And the bride and groom would be there. She might get some more ideas about exactly what they wanted. Details could make all the difference between a spectacular cake and a truly stunning one. Technically, it would even count as a business meeting with her main client.

"It won't take long," Clay assured her. "You can just help me gloat shamelessly about our victory and then we'll be on our way."

His persistence eroded her will to say no.

"Sure. Why not."

"I have to say—" he dramatically clasped a hand to his chest "—your lack of enthusiasm when it comes to spending time with me is a bit ego-crushing."

She had to laugh at that. If he only knew... "I apologize for my rudeness. I would love to join you for a drink with your sister and future brother-in-law." She bowed slightly for effect.

"That's more like it," he teased.

After Tori ran into a nearby restroom to throw some cold water on her sweaty face and tidy her frazzled hair, she met Clay where he waited at a high-top table in the far corner of the tavern.

She approached just as his phone dinged with a text.

"Good thing I didn't wait for them to order," he said as he read the message.

"What's going on?"

He held up the phone for her. "My sister informs me that they've run into a delay and are running late to meet us."

Tori could think of all sorts of reasons why a bride and groom might run into a delay after stopping in their hotel room. But she figured Clay probably didn't want to think about that, being the bride's brother and all.

A server appeared with a sweaty bottle of beer and a full, frosty glass of white wine.

"I figured you'd want something cold and ordered you a chardonnay. We can send it back if you'd like something else."

"This is perfect. Thank you." In fact, her mouth was watering for a taste of refreshment. It had gotten quite hot out there on the court. By the third game, she'd felt like a sweaty mess with frizzy, tangled hair.

Clay, by contrast, had managed to appear impeccable throughout the whole match, even with beads of sweat rolling down his cheeks and glistening along his arms.

Another text alert sounded on his phone and Tori could guess what it said.

Clay confirmed her assumptions. "Gemma again. They've decided to bag it altogether. They won't be joining us, after all."

He lifted his glass to her in a mini salute. "Looks like it's just you and me."

He noticed something that might be described as alarm flickered behind Tori's eyes. She recovered quickly, however, saying, "That's too bad. I wanted to talk to them some more about their cake."

Did that explain why she'd looked so alarmed when she'd heard Gemma and Tom wouldn't be joining them, after all? Or was it something else?

Clay couldn't deny there seemed to be an undercurrent between them. Almost like an ethereal crackling in the air. Was Tori aware of it, too? Maybe it was all in his head.

He studied her as she took a small sip of her wine. She was still flushed from their game. Already, her skin had developed a slight tan. Her lips were moist from the chilled wine.

Another thing he couldn't deny was how attracted he was to her. She possessed an underlying strength that seemed at odds with her sweet and soft demeanor. The contrast called to him in a way he couldn't recall ever experiencing before.

The problem was, he had no business thinking about any of this. And he'd certainly had no business pulling her into his arms and holding her close the way he had on the tennis court. Heaven help him, all he'd wanted to do after putting her back on her feet was to lift her chin, pull her face to his and take those tempting, full lips with his own. And he might have done just that if they'd been alone. Thank goodness they hadn't been.

He was much too damaged for a woman the likes of Victoria Preston. A fact he'd do well to remember.

Clay's musings were interrupted when the server reappeared by their side. He carried a wide, ceramic platter full of food that he placed between them on the table. "Cracked conch with various dipping sauces," he announced. "An island specialty. On the house for our esteemed guests."

The enticing aroma of the fried seafood had his stomach grumbling and he felt almost grateful for the distraction.

"That looks delicious," Tori told the waiter with a warm smile. "Thank you."

The man looked ready to melt at the smile she gave him.

Welcome to the club, buddy.

"I didn't think I was hungry until he brought this out." He motioned for her to go ahead. "Ladies first."

Tori gingerly lifted a small piece then dipped it into a small cup of sauce. As she bit into it, her eyes grew wide and she let out a soft moan.

Clay had to grip the table to keep from reacting. "I take it it's good?"

"Heavenly. I'll have to see if I can wrangle the recipe to share with my mom. Wait till you try one!"

He almost didn't want to take any, just to watch her savor every last morsel. In the end, though, his stomach won out.

She was right. The conch melted in his mouth as a burst of flavor exploded on his tongue.

"Oh man. That is good." He pointed to the dipping sauce he'd just used. "You have to taste that one next."

Tori did as he suggested, her reaction instantaneous and just as visceral as the last time. Her eyelids lowered as her tongue darted out to lick her lower lip.

Sweet mercy.

He was going to have to look away. He might have to ask the waiter to turn the television on. Just so he had something else to focus on. Had any woman he'd ever encountered looked so sexy while she ate?

An image popped into his head before he could so much as stop it. He'd picked up a morsel of food and was feeding it to Tori. He could feel those luscious lips around his finger as she took in the bite—

Clay sucked in a breath.

A television wasn't going to help. He doubted even a cold shower might. Yet he still couldn't make himself look away. When she took another bite of food, a small drop of sauce landed on her chin, right below her lip. The gods were surely laughing at him with all the temptation they kept throwing his way.

He knew he shouldn't, but he couldn't seem to help himself. It was like asking him not to take his next breath. He leaned over to indicate the exact spot. "You, uh, missed your mouth with some of that."

"Huh?"

He lifted his hand to point out exactly where the sauce had dripped on her chin. Only he did more than point. His hand seemed to move on its own. Before he knew it, he was wiping the sauce away with his thumb. Her skin felt soft and smooth under his finger.

She gasped at his touch but made no move to shift away.

Another vision appeared in his mind. He was leaning closer, replacing his finger with his tongue. He imagined tasting her. He was sure she would taste of salt and sea and spice.

Man. This is bad. Totally wrong.

He couldn't be lusting after a friendly baker he'd only seen once or twice when an occasion called for it. What was the matter with him? He usually had a better hold on his libido.

He'd been without female companionship for too long. That's all this craziness was. But he couldn't seem to bring himself to move away, and his hand was still lingering on her face. Would it be so wrong to stroke her cheek? To gently grasp the tendril of hair that had fallen out of the elastic and tuck it back behind her ear?

Would he be able to stop himself once he started touching her, knowing it was the wrong thing to do? After all, he'd had to force himself to let her go after embracing her on the court.

It didn't help matters that Tori still hadn't made any kind of move to back away from his touch. Her breath warmed the skin of his hand. Her breathing had gone ragged and sharp.

A commotion from the direction of the doorway scattered his attention, breaking the moment. A gaggle of bikini-clad young women noisily entered the tavern and headed to the bar area. The disruption brought Clay to his senses. And not a moment too soon. He immediately dropped his hand and reached for another piece of conch.

Tori blinked twice and shifted in her chair to lean back.

He wasn't imagining it or reading into things. She was clearly as attracted to him as he was to her. And what was he to do with that information?

Of course, the only sane answer was to ignore it.

So that's what if felt like. To feel true desire, to tremble with temptation. To want a man as much as she wanted her next breath. Tori realized she'd never really experienced such a fierce longing for a man, despite having been in a years-long relationship.

In fact, she'd never experienced anything like this with Drew. Certainly not toward the end. No, she'd felt nothing then but trepidation and something akin to fear the more time they'd spent together. As each argument grew louder and scarier than the last... As each of his criticisms, on everything from her clothing to her hairstyle, became more and more insulting... He'd chipped away at her sense of self and security until desire was the last thing she felt toward the man.

No, she'd never felt for Drew what she was currently experiencing with Clay.

She sat stunned and disoriented at what had just transpired between them. For a moment there, she could have sworn that Clay was going to lean in and kiss her. And, heaven help her, she would have let him. More than that, she would have welcomed it.

She'd have kissed him back.

What would it feel like to kiss Clayton Ramos? As it was, the mere touch of his thumb on her chin had her quaking inside. Her face still felt hot, her cheeks burned. Her breath caught in her throat.

Snap out of it.

Regardless of what had just happened between them— or almost happened—she was here as Clay's employee. She couldn't let herself lose sight of that fact. They were in paradise. For a fantasy wedding, no less. The very atmosphere they found themselves in was ripe for tempting and romantic thoughts. A dangerous combination given how she'd harbored a crush on the man since first laying eyes on him.

But none of that was real. A reality she couldn't ignore, because reality would hit her soon enough, like immediately after she landed on US soil. Back in Boston, once all this was over, she'd return to a life of baking specialty cake orders and making cupcakes, along with occasionally working the random shift as needed at her family's restaurant. Without any certain knowledge of when she might even see Clay again. And he would probably forget her very existence until he needed another layered cake.

Tori refused to spend any time pining after a man she could never have. She wouldn't subject herself to a life committed to sitting by the phone waiting for a call that may never come.

And what would it do to her heart to see him with another woman? To watch him on various tabloid websites accompany someone else to the latest premiere?

She'd worked much too hard to build a life she found fulfilling and enjoyable. A life that merited her full focus. She owed herself that much.

Tori lifted her gaze upward to find him studying her face.

"Tori?" He said her name so softly, it bordered on a whisper. She knew full well the question he was asking. But she was nowhere near ready to answer it.

Making quick work of finishing the rest of her wine, she gave him a polite smile. "I really should get back to that sketch now."

Then, erring on the side of rudeness, she hopped off the stool and made herself walk away.

She heard him bite out a curse as she left.

CHAPTER FOUR

"THERE YOU ARE." Gemma's familiar voice sounded from behind her on the beach. Tori carefully placed the cupcake tower on the picnic table set up for desserts. The early evening sky was just starting to dim as a soft tropical wind breezed through the air.

Gemma reached her side. "Wow. That's a work of art."

"Thanks."

"I'm so tempted to just snare one of those right now rather than after dinner." She pointed to the middle layer. "Is that one key lime?"

"It is," Tori answered. "And I won't tell a soul should you have dessert before dinner."

Gemma giggled. "I'll be good. This time."

"Were you looking for me?"

"Yes. I wanted to make sure you knew to join us for dinner."

What a totally unexpected offer. Tori really had no intention of doing anything but hanging in her hotel room with a glass of wine and the paperback she'd picked up at the airport. She opened her mouth to argue but Gemma cut her off. "I insist."

It didn't seem right. She had no hope of avoiding Clay if she was to attend a beachside picnic dinner as if she were a regular guest. "Gemma, I couldn't impose that way."

Her eyebrows lifted. "Impose? We're tennis pals, remember. You just happen to be baking for me."

Tori couldn't help but be touched by her words. But there was still the question of Clay. She wasn't sure if she could act unaffected where he was concerned. Not after what had happened in the tavern after their tennis match. And the chances of avoiding him were probably slim to none at a beachside dinner.

Gemma threw down the proverbial gauntlet. "I'm the bride and what I say goes."

It was hard to argue that point.

About twenty minutes later, Tori found herself heading to the beach against her better judgment, in a red flowery summer dress and black canvas sandals. She'd packed exactly two dressy outfits, not really imagining she would need them, but was now glad she had.

Her heart nearly stopped when she saw him.

Wearing loose cotton pants and a short-sleeved shirt unbuttoned at the neck, he exuded the perfect picture of a virile, handsome male. Walking from the direction of the residence cottages, she could tell even from this distance that his hair was wet, making it look a shade darker. It brought out the chocolate brown of his eyes.

A toddler in a white-lace dress darted out from nowhere and made a beeline for Clay. Tori watched with amusement as the tot wrapped herself around his shin. Without pause, he bent to retrieve her and swung her around in a circle. Tori could hear the little girl's giggles loud and clear despite the crashing of the waves behind her. Then, planting an affectionate kiss on her cheek, Clay set the toddler atop his shoulders.

"That's Lilly. Our niece." Gemma had come to stand beside her without Tori even noticing. No wonder, her gaze and focus had been completely on the man who so thoroughly seemed to demand her attention whenever he was present.

"She's almost three," Gemma said.

The pieces fell into place in Tori's mind. Lilly's mother had to be the other sister. Adria. The one whose wedding she'd created a cake for just about three years ago. Given the new information, she could definitely see the family resemblance. Lilly had the same nose and coloring of her mother's side of the family.

"She's absolutely adorable."

"And she knows it because we all spoil her rotten." Gemma pointed in her brother's direction. "Particularly that one there."

She so didn't need to be hearing about Clay as a doting uncle. Nor did she need to be seeing it firsthand. The picture was doing nothing to abate her patently inconvenient and ever-growing attraction.

Tori made herself look away and turn fully to face Gemma, to try to change the subject. As if she had any hope of getting her mind off of Clay Ramos in any way.

"The food looks divine." It smelled pretty good, too. Trays of barbecued meats, various pasta dishes and tropical salads with exotic fruits and vegetables had been set up on half a dozen wooden tables.

"So does your cupcake tower," Gemma said graciously. "You're very talented."

Tori had heard that before, but never tired of having clients remind her they thought so. "Thanks."

"For that matter, you're not a bad tennis player, either." She gave her a playful nudge. "Clay wouldn't have stood a chance at winning if it weren't for you. You should tell him I said so."

No part of that statement was true. Tori spread her hands and shook her head. "Oh no. No way I'm getting in the middle of any kind of sibling rivalry."

Gemma chuckled. "Well, Tom and I have been thinking, and we've decided we'd like a rematch."

Tori laughed. "Is that so? I'll consider it. And Clay will have to agree, of course." That was a fib. Tori had no intention whatsoever of playing partner to Clay in any way, shape or form. Not again. Her psyche couldn't handle the proximity or the temptation.

"You and my brother make a good team," Gemma declared, taking her gently by the forearm. "Here, you can sit next to him at our table."

Tori Preston sure cleaned up well. Clay had to force himself not to stare outright as she walked with Gemma from the buffet area set up by the water.

Dressed in a loose-fitting, spaghetti-strapped red dress that brought out the bright color of her eyes and fell just above her knees, she looked like a vision straight out of the dreams of any red-blooded male. Including himself.

How had he not noticed how shapely her legs were before now? She looked the part of an innocent yet alluring seductress who had no idea just how seductive she was. He wasn't the only one who noticed. Glancing around the beach, Clay could see she was attracting all sorts of attention. More than one pair of male eyes followed her as the two women made their way over. His gut tautened in annoyance.

Funny, he'd never considered himself to be the jealous type before this very moment.

He set his niece on her feet on the sand and gave her a small tickle under her chin. The child ran back to her mother with a delightful squeal of laughter.

Tori smiled at Lilly as the little girl darted by and he noticed that her hair seemed softer. She'd toned the spikes into delicate curls that framed her face.

And since when had he been the type to note changes in a woman's hairstyle? Tori Preston was bringing out a side of him he hardly recognized. A side he didn't want to examine too closely. Or even acknowledge.

He'd experienced firsthand the dire ramifications that could arise when lovesick souls followed their desires without regard to the end results. Without regard to the effect their actions would have on those around them.

He was smarter than that. He would never allow such basic needs or desires to change who he was at his core. Not like the parent who had utterly betrayed him and his siblings.

Clay pushed away the unpleasant wayward thoughts. This was to be a celebratory night, after all. He may as well try to enjoy it.

He hadn't expected to see Tori here, but her presence was a pleasant surprise. No offense to his lovely sister, but beachside dinner parties weren't exactly his kind of scene. But suddenly the hours ahead were looking quite a bit more promising.

At least he'd have someone engaging to talk to. Most of the guests were either Gemma's or Tom's friends. Other than immediate family and a handful of cousins he hadn't seen in ages, there was no one he would exactly call a friend or even an associate. And he was growing tired of small talk with people he didn't know from random strangers on the street.

In fact, the only person in attendance he'd directly invited was an officer of the charity Clay had founded—an outreach program for underprivileged kids in the Boston area.

"Look who I convinced to join us," Gemma said with a warm smile once they reached his side.

"Why, it's my lovely doubles partner. Has

my sister informed you she's challenged us to a rematch?"

Tori laughed and the sound of it had his smile widening. He'd never been one to wax poetic, but she really did have a face that lit up whenever she smiled.

Oh man. Get a grip on yourself.

His sister was looking at him funny, the corners of her lips trembling ever so slightly. He didn't even want to know what she found so amusing. He'd have to be sure to set her straight if she was harboring any illusions that something might be brewing between him and the baker hired for her wedding.

Gemma should know him better than that.

Around them, several tiki torches were being lit one by one.

"That's our cue that all the food is out," Gemma informed them. "If you'll excuse me, I'll go let folks know they can begin eating. Clay, would you mind showing Tori to our table after you two get your plates?"

Subtle, she was not.

"Looks like you're stuck with me," he said with a wink when his sister left.

"And vice versa."

Tori appeared tense, less than comfortable. Was she thinking about their drink in the tavern earlier? Heaven knew he hadn't been able to get those moments out of his mind. But there was no reason they couldn't behave like mature adults. A few unguarded moments this afternoon didn't have to define or mar the rest of the evening. And the last thing he wanted was for Tori to be uncomfortable around him.

First, he had to somehow break the ice between them. "I'm not all that hungry yet. Though I could use a drink. How about you?"

"That'd be nice. Thanks."

He took her gently by the elbow and led her to the poolside cabana bar several feet away. The evening's specialty drink was a coconut rum punch and Clay ordered one for each of them. The infinity pool was aglow with soft, neon lights from within. Several more tiki torches surrounded the area around the crystal-blue water.

After getting their drinks, he led her to a pair of poolside chaise longues.

"So what's the full story about your sister? How did you happen to just stumble upon a long-lost twin?" He paused. "I can't believe I just actually asked that question."

Tori's soft chuckle echoed slightly in the air. "It happens to be the truth."

"Please tell."

"My friend Josh—I told you about him on the boat ride to the island, remember?"

Clay remembered, all right. He remembered all too well the twinge of jealousy he'd felt until she'd clarified that they were nothing more than friends. "I do."

"Well, he came across a picture of a young woman who bore a striking resemblance to the sister of his two closest friends. Me." She pointed to her chest as if there was any doubt who she was referring to. "When he showed me the pic, it was like a missing piece of a puzzle fell into place. I suddenly had an answer to questions I didn't even realize were nagging at me."

Her eyes glittered with excitement as she continued. "Josh had a business trip planned to Australia—where she lived then—so I asked him to check her out. What happened next was straight out of a fairy tale. Eloise and Josh fell madly in love and, after a few bumps in the road, decided they couldn't live without each other. They were recently married in a beautiful ceremony."

"Huh." That was all Clay could manage as a response. What a remarkable tale. The woman sitting before him was fascinating in myriad ways. He'd never met anyone like her.

Tori jutted her chin toward the crowded buffet. "I hope we're not being antisocial."

He shrugged. "It's hard to be social with people you haven't even met yet."

Both eyebrows quirked. "You don't know most of them?"

He shook his head. "Not really. Gemma and Tom created the guest list and picked the venue. In fact, I only invited one of the guests here. If we're not including you, that is."

"Just the one, huh?"

He nodded. "I mostly just write the checks."

She was silent, playing with her cardboard straw and swirling the ice at the bottom of her glass.

Clay felt compelled to explain. "My future brother-in-law is a graduate student with a boatload of student loans. He insists he'll pay me back as soon as he's solvent. I won't accept it, of course, but I appreciate his desire to do so. The man is a brilliant engineer and studying something I can't pronounce at MIT."

"Sounds like you're okay with the man your sister is about to bond herself with."

He chuckled. "Yeah. I guess I am. Don't understand why anyone would want to get married in the first place, but Tom's a good guy. He'll be a welcome addition to the family. Lord knows we need some good character to make up for—" He stopped. Tori was easy to talk to, and he was letting himself be carried away, but there was no use delving into the past. And he certainly didn't want to dampen the mood of the evening by rehashing all that unpleasantness. Nothing good ever came of looking backward, after all.

There really was no point in dredging up memories of how his life had been completely upended after the loss of his father. Or the way his mother had let him and his sisters down time after time.

All that was water under the bridge.

"I beg your pardon?" she asked after waiting several beats for him to continue.

"Never mind," he answered. "It's not important. You haven't tried it yet." He gestured to the glass she held.

Tori took a tentative sip of her drink. Her eyes widened. "Oh my."

He laughed at her reaction. "Good?"

"Dangerously good."

He chuckled. "Dangerous, huh?"

"Yes, tasty but strong. It would be much too easy to overindulge if not paying attention."

He got the impression she didn't indulge very often, didn't often let her guard down. It surprised him how badly he wanted to be the one to somehow change that about her.

But that was wishful thinking. The sweet, pretty pastry chef was off limits and out of his league.

* * *

So, he was something of a loner.

The revelation surprised Tori. All the parties he was photographed attending, all those high-society soirées with a beautiful woman draped on his arm—it all painted a much different picture than the man she was starting to get to know.

The fact that he was here solo was also pretty telling. Not that she had any business speculating about his personal life. Given his reputation as a ladies' man, it was more than clear where he stood on things such as marriage and commitment. Apparently, the only thing Clay was committed to was remaining a bachelor. And if that thought had her bemoaning reality, well then, that was her issue, wasn't it?

Polishing off the tropical drinks, they made their way over to the festivities and grabbed two plates of heaping food before heading for the table. Clay's being a bit more heaping than hers.

Tori was happy to see the cupcake tower almost empty. People were not waiting to finish their meal before grabbing their dessert.

In Clay's case, he wasn't even waiting to eat dessert. The first thing he bit into when he sat was her key lime concoction with citrus-cream filling. Closing his eyes, he took a deep breath. "You are a magician. This should be criminally banned it's so good."

The sheer enthusiasm of his compliment sent warmth through her body. She had to acknowledge she was actually having a really good time. It had been at least two years since she'd been at any kind of social event that didn't involve the bakery or her parents.

In fact, the last time she'd been at any kind of party had been with Drew. Toward the end, any time spent with him had felt obligatory and stressful. She'd been so afraid of saying or doing the wrong thing around him, she'd constantly walked on eggshells. It was so tense that, after a while, Tori had simply become accustomed to feeling coiled like a tight spring whenever they were together. She'd almost forgotten what if felt like to just enjoy herself. No small factor in all of this, she had to admit, was that Clay had a way of putting her at ease.

The coconut drink by the pool earlier also didn't hurt. Now, with a plate of delicious and exotic food in front of her, another tropical drink, and the rhythmic notes of calypso in the air, she felt more at ease then she had in months. Maybe even years.

Too bad it was all so temporary.

* * *

Thirty minutes after they'd taken their seats, Tom and Gemma stood and called for attention.

"All right, everyone, it's time for the entertainment portion of the evening," Tom announced. "First, we're starting off with some fun and games. Followed by a night of dancing with the island's most popular DJ."

Gemma took over. "And we're going to kick it off with some competitive fun. Grab a partner and join us by the water for a bag toss contest. There'll be prizes for the winners."

A split second of panic shot through Tori at the word "partner." The last thing she wanted was for Clay to feel obligated to spend the whole evening with her playing beach games. She turned to tell him so, but before she could so much as speak, he gently took her by the wrist and guided her up.

"Come on, I want one of those prizes."

Tori felt laughter bubble up her throat. "Do you even have any idea what the prizes are?"

He shook his head. "Not a clue."

"Then why the mad dash?"

He shrugged. "What can I say? I have a competitive streak."

She let him tug her toward the activity, unable to hold her laughter. "Wait. There's something you should know before this goes any further."

"What's that?"

"I draw the line at three-legged races."

He scoffed. "No promises. I'll carry you if I have to."

The image that statement prompted sent a bolt of excitement through her chest and brought forth memories of the way he'd held her after they'd played tennis.

She absolutely could not go there. She'd spent most of the day trying to convince herself that her reaction had been nothing more than reflex and had no basis in anything authentic.

Clay was an attractive man oozing with sex appeal. And she'd simply had a natural reaction to being the target of his charms. Who could blame her?

Their opponents turned out to be Tom's college roommate and his fiancée—Steve and Brenda. They were an attractive couple who weren't exactly shying away from physical affection, their arms wrapped around each other's waists as they started to play. Tori felt a pang of longing that took her by surprise at the picture they presented.

"You go first, Tori," Clay prompted, distracting her from the disquieting thought and handing her a small beanbag.

Though she did her best, when she tossed it, the bag landed nowhere near the target hole. In fact, it landed perilously close to the water and was nearly swept away on a wave. Clay dashed to catch it just in time.

He groaned as he returned to stand next to her, and Tori's heart sank. It was just a silly game, but she remembered how Drew could become so disappointed with her at times. Even when it came to silly games. Nothing was lighthearted where Drew was concerned.

She swallowed and turned to apologize, to vow that she would try to do better with her next toss.

But Clay didn't look disappointed. He looked amused. And the grin he gave her had her heart jumping in her chest. "That was a bad toss, sweetheart," he told her, topping off the statement with a wink.

Tori felt the relief clear to her toes. She shrugged at him. "Oops."

In the end, they lost soundly, but they managed to win the next event, a couples' beach volleyball game. Their winnings consisted of a helium balloon and a bottle of chilled white wine, which Clay explained wasn't really any kind of prize at all, seeing as all food and beverage was already paid for.

By him.

Clay handed her the wine after the game. "This belongs to you," he said with an exaggerated bow.

"We won it together," she argued.

"That we did. But I insist you take it. A token symbolizing our triumph."

She thanked him and took the sweaty bottle. To think, she hadn't even wanted to be here tonight. But she couldn't recall the last time she'd enjoyed herself quite as much. It had been a while since she'd felt so relaxed and been able to just let go and play. She'd forgotten what it was like to be carefree. The fun-loving, lighthearted girl she'd once been had been slowly and determinedly crushed. And though she was working on it, rediscovering that girl was proving to be tougher than she would have liked. It was going to take some time and effort.

What better opportunity to do so than a night like tonight? She was in the Bahamas playing beach games! Without anyone judging her, or making her feel less than. She could laugh as loud as she wanted, let her hair down and thoroughly enjoy herself. There was no one here to look down on her or to ridicule her for letting loose a little. It would be a wonder if she could even remember how after so many years of being stifled and put down.

A wave of bitterness threatened to wash over her when she thought of just how much of her natural personality she'd squelched all those years she'd been with Drew.

But bitterness wasn't going to restore what she'd lost during that time. And she'd vowed to do just that. To rediscover who she'd once been before the ill-fated relationship that had only managed to dampen her spirit and almost crush her soul. She owed it to that young woman she'd once been to try to bring her back. In full form. No, bitterness was the last thing she needed to be focused on right now.

So she focused on Clay instead.

"All these activities call for people partnering up. I bet you're sorry you didn't bring anyone along, aren't you?" she teased, her voice bubbling with laughter.

His eyes suddenly darkened and the air between them grew thick. "Actually, I think it might have been the best decision I've made in as long as I can remember."

Right then Tori realized that, for one of the very few times in her life, she knew exactly what she wanted, despite the fact that every sane sense she possessed was screaming to her that it was oh so wrong. She wanted Clay to kiss her. It didn't even matter that they were surrounded by others. It didn't matter that she knew no one here and barely knew the man himself. She wanted to feel his lips on hers.

And she wanted it with every fiber of her being.

How many times in the span of a day could a man feel an overwhelming desire to pull someone into his arms and kiss her senseless?

Clay could see in Tori's eyes that was also exactly what she wanted. It was clear as the full Bahamian moon above them.

Also clear was the fact that he had no business thinking such thoughts at all. Tori wasn't the type any decent man would entertain indulging in a fling with, knowing he would then walk away. And he simply didn't have it in him to offer anyone much more than that. His years simply trying to survive and ensuring that his sisters did so, as well, had taken too much out of him. There were days he barely felt like more than a shell.

Someone like that had no business even entertaining the idea of any kind of real relationship.

If only things were different. If reality wasn't what it was, he would be thanking his lucky stars that he'd run into Tori Preston and he'd be moving heaven and earth to be able to call himself her man. But his father's death served as a marker that delineated the before and after that defined Clay's life.

Maybe if his father had survived, Clay would have grown into the kind of man whose future included someone like Tori. But fate had thrown tragedy his way at such a young age.

So it made no sense that, instead of bidding her good-night and walking away, he reached his hand out to her when the DJ started the first song.

"Dance with me?"

She hesitated just long enough that he thought she might turn him down. Part of him felt a flood of relief—at least one of them was showing a lick of sense. A bigger part felt like someone might have kicked him in the teeth.

Finally, she slipped her palm into his and walked with him onto the makeshift dance area where several couples were already bouncing and swaying to the upbeat reggae tune.

"It's been a while since I've gone dancing," Tori whispered in his ear over the music. Like it was some sort of confession.

"Oh? Operating your own successful business must take a lot of your time."

She looked away but made no further comment. Was he imagining it or was there something in the way she was moving so stiffly, as if she were holding herself back?

It seemed uncharacteristic. She was the last woman he would have pegged as rigid or wooden in any sense.

It took some time, but Tori eventually seemed to loosen up.

And then he couldn't think at all. All he could do was stare openmouthed like some caveman at the way she began to move. Tori lifted both arms above her head and began swaying her hips in such an alluring tease, he felt his mouth go dry. Her expression went from guarded and cautious to one of near abandon. The transformation made Clay want to grab the nearest icy drink and pour it over his head to cool himself down. He tried to shift his gaze and somehow shut his mouth as she continued to move to the music. His efforts were futile. His fingers itched to reach for her, to pull her tempting, swaying hips up against him and move with her until they found a rhythm all their own.

Perhaps jumping in the pool would be more effective.

Two songs later, someone above must have finally taken mercy on him. The next song was blessedly slow and he took her in his arms without thinking. His relief didn't last long, for now they were slow dancing. The touch of her soft, supple body up tight against his length was just further sweet agony.

He tried for conversation as a distraction.

"For someone who hasn't danced in a while, you sure don't seem to be at a loss for moves."

Her gasp was sudden and audible. She pulled back to look at him. Her eyes had grown wide with something akin to near panic. "I'm so sorry."

He blinked in confusion. "What in the world are you apologizing for? That was meant as a compliment."

"It was?"

How could she not see that?

She released a heavy breath. "So, I didn't embarrass you?"

Embarrassed? That was the last thing he'd been feeling while watching her dance.

In fact, he was certain he'd been the envy of most of the men present. Was he missing something?

"You most definitely didn't embarrass me. Not in any way, shape or form."

Her shoulders visibly slumped with relief. "I didn't?"

"Of course not. Why would you even think that?"

She chewed her bottom lip. "I've been told once or twice in the past that I can be a bit… unreserved at times. Particularly on the dance floor."

Huh. The thought wouldn't have crossed his mind. That would certainly explain why she hadn't been dancing in a while.

"Who in the world told you that?"

She looked away again. "Someone I was close to once. Not too long ago."

He put two and two together. "Boyfriend?"

She swallowed then nodded slowly. "An ex."

Silently, he pulled her back into his arms and began swaying with her once more.

Said ex-boyfriend had certainly done a number on her. Clay'd never had such an overwhelming rush of ire toward a faceless man he'd never met.

A frustrating jumble of emotions had his chest cramping. Rage that anyone had ever made her feel less in any way. Bafflement at the nameless former boyfriend who clearly hadn't appreciated what he'd had. And something else he couldn't quite name. Something he refused to acknowledge as protectiveness. Maybe the caveman description was more accurate than not.

Tori's eyes had grown shiny in moonlight. He lifted her chin, struggling for the right words. "I don't see how someone like you could ever be embarrassing, Tori. And certainly not for something as simple as enjoying yourself on the dance floor."

Her answer was to nestle closer against him as they continued to dance.

The next song was a faster, hip-hop beat but Clay didn't bother to alter his tempo. Tori made no move to, either.

What man in his right mind would want to stop her from doing what he'd just witnessed? Or want to try to tamp her joy or exuberance in any way?

He wanted so badly to find out.

Tori didn't know how much time had passed. Or how many romantically slow songs the DJ had even played up till now. She only knew it felt right to be held by Clay Ramos, to sway slowly in his arms. Time stood still when he held her. The rest of the world seemed to disappear.

He made her feel safe, coveted. Even as she'd told him about the uncomfortable experience she'd had with her ex-boyfriend.

But she didn't want to think about Drew. She didn't want to give him the power to mar this magical night any more than he already had. In fact, she regretted having mentioned him at all.

Clearly, she'd overreacted. But Clay's comment about her dancing had just sent a flood of insecurities gushing through her core and the old familiar serpent of self-doubt had slithered in. How many times had she been told that she was drawing too much attention? Doubt that Drew had been right all those times—that she could be too uninhibited at the wrong moment, that she was never serious enough—had resurfaced without warning. Clearly, Tori had more work to do rediscovering herself than she might have thought.

Until he'd explained, it hadn't even occurred to Tori that Clay may have been actually complimenting her on something she'd been told to rein in so often in the past.

A woman could get used to such compliments.

The now familiar aroma of Clay's aftershave settled around her, an enticing combination of sandalwood and mint. She might have to come up with a recipe inspired by those scents when she got back to Boston.

Not a good idea.

Because she'd be back in Boston soon enough. And then what? All of the magic she was experiencing right now would be nothing but a dream of memory. On second thought, the best thing for her to do once she returned to real life would be to forget about Clay altogether. His scent, his compliments, the warmth of his skin.

She'd be better off pretending he didn't even exist. The last thing she needed was to be reminded of the way Clay had made her feel when he'd held her on a makeshift dance floor on a warm, breezy evening in the Bahamas one fairy-tale night.

No, far better for her to remind herself that this had just been some fantasy she may very well have made up. Then she could move on with her life, pretend none of it had ever really happened.

For the sake of her heart.

CHAPTER FIVE

TWO HOURS AFTER his first song, the DJ bade everyone a good night and started packing up. The activities over, the guests slowly started to disperse.

Tori felt a pang of disappointment. She didn't want the evening to end just yet. Though maybe it was a good thing. She hadn't intended to reveal quite so much of herself to Clay. On the dance floor, no less. In her defense, she found him easy to confide in, someone who listened without judgment. Aside from her sister, whom she'd only just found, Tori couldn't think of anyone else who had ever made her feel so understood when it came to her insecurities. Shawna was a dear friend, but often she could be too quick to try to offer advice or solutions when simply offering a shoulder to lean on would do.

Slowly, Clay released his hold around her and reluctantly she stepped away.

"Looks like the party's over." His voice sounded gravelly, forced. Would it be wishful thinking to imagine he wanted the night to continue, as well?

Tori couldn't remember a time she'd been so tempted by a man. And that said a lot about her previous relationship.

Stop it.

She really had no business comparing the two men. Clay and Drew didn't have a thing in common. In fact, she couldn't really compare Clay to anyone. He really was a special kind of man. Gentle, kind, a good listener. Not to mention his professional success and his devotion to his sisters.

Almost too good to be true.

And perhaps he was. Tori couldn't discount the role that the sheer novelty of the situation might be playing on her perceptions overall. A tropical island, the romantic setting of a wedding, the way they kept being thrown together… It all made for a heady combination.

"Don't forget your trophy." He pointed to the wine bottle that sat at the nearest table. "I'll walk you back to your room."

"You don't need to bother."

"It's not a bother, Tori. In fact, it would be my pleasure."

Spoken like a true gentleman. Something

she'd forgotten existed. It would take some getting used to. "In that case, I'd appreciate the company."

She picked up the wine bottle on their way toward the residence area.

"Do you mind if we walk along the beach? It's such a beautiful night," he asked, surprising her with the question.

She couldn't agree more. The moon had floated gradually higher above the clouds, casting a silvery glow on the white sand. In the distance, the water looked like an ocean of black ink. The horizon was the color of rich regal velvet. It would be a shame to head indoors now on such a night as this. Plus, she was all for prolonging the evening a little longer.

When they reached the water, she took her sandals off and gripped them in her free hand. He reached for them immediately. "Here, I'll carry those. You have enough of a load with that wine."

A gentleman in more ways than one. No wonder the ladies seemed to adore him, even the little ones. "Your niece is adorable, by the way," she said, recalling the little girl and how thrilled she'd seemed at the attention of her uncle.

His face visibly brightened at the mention

of the little girl. "Thanks, it's been good to see Lilly again. It's been a while."

"Oh? Why's that?"

His smile faltered. "Adria and I have hit a bit of a rough patch due to a…disagreement, so to speak."

"I'm sorry to hear that. And at such a joyous time."

Tori wished she could soothe him somehow, just as he had managed to soothe her when she'd confided so much of herself as they'd danced.

The sheer dismay in his voice tugged at her heart. Whatever had happened between him and his sister, it was affecting him on a deep level.

He released a heavy sigh. "We'll get past it. It's just going to take some time."

A relatively high wave splashed at her shins, soaking the bottom of her dress. Tucking the bottle under her arm, she fashioned a makeshift knot of the wet fabric to keep the dampness off her skin. "Do you want to talk about it?" she asked, straightening.

The muscles around his jaw grew taut. "It was just a disagreement about the guest list." He paused then added, "More or less."

Tori had the impression it was probably more

the former. "I thought you said you weren't really involved in who was invited."

He shrugged. "I wasn't, really. I just have a strong opinion about one guest in particular. I didn't want her to have any part of this wedding celebration. Adria disagreed." He sounded utterly perplexed by the fact.

She wondered if he was speaking of an ex. Her guess would be that he'd dated someone his sister was friends with and it hadn't ended well. Jealousy prickled along her skin at the thought. But the theory made sense, didn't it? That would explain why he was here solo, why he'd bickered with his sister about one guest in particular.

"Wouldn't Gemma have the ultimate say?" she ventured. "It is her wedding, after all."

He shook his head. "She wanted nothing to do with the disagreement, and I can't blame her for wanting to stay out of it. She ordered Adria and me to work it out between us."

That clearly hadn't happened. Tori wondered if Adria had won out, if there was an ex-girlfriend of Clay's on the island. Perhaps Tori had even walked by her without having a clue as to who she was or what she might have meant to him before they'd broken up. The jealousy she didn't want to acknowledge ratcheted up several notches.

She wasn't going to ask him, refused to pry. Even though her curiosity was so strong, she could almost taste it in the back of her throat.

Turned out she didn't need to.

Clay huffed out a long sigh. "Adria wanted someone to attend who I no longer want to have any interaction with in this lifetime." Every muscle in Clay's body seemed to vibrate with tension and anger. Whoever he was referring to had clearly hurt him deeply and in a way that had left a lasting mark.

Tori held her breath, willing him to say more while at the same time afraid to hear there might be another woman on this very island who apparently had meant a great deal to him at some point in time.

He waited a beat before finally adding, "Our mother."

Tori bit back her gasp of surprise. Her guess hadn't even been close.

All this time, Tori had just figured Clay and his sisters had lost their parents. After all, there hadn't been a mother of the bride in attendance at any of the cake design or tasting visits for either Adria's or Gemma's wedding.

"My mother has been estranged from all of us for several years now," Clay explained, shedding some light on the mystery. "Adria suddenly wanted to see if she could change that. I don't."

"I see."

A slight chill had settled in the breezy air, though the water at her feet still felt balmy and warm. "What about your father?" Tori asked.

Clay's shoulders visibly slumped. "We lost him years ago. I was twelve."

Judging by the way the mere mention of his father completely deflated him, Tori had no doubt the two had been close. She couldn't imagine life without either of her parents. Even as an adult, the loss of her mother or father would completely shatter her. Her heart was breaking for the boy Clay must have been, trying to cope with so much grief at such a tender age. Just as he was about to enter the formative and angst-filled teen years. Heaven knew, her own teenage experience had held more drama than she would have cared for. But she'd had it easy compared to Clay and his sisters.

Nothing could parallel the loss of a beloved parent. "I'm so sorry, Clay."

"Thank you for saying that."

"Life can be so cruel and unfair sometimes."

He nodded and looked off into the horizon. "In a way, we lost my mother then, too. She became a completely different woman."

"People can be withdrawn or unavailable

while dealing with their own grief." She recalled when her maternal grandmother had passed away. Her mom had rushed to Sicily to be by her side. Marissa had been a grief-stricken, unrecognizable version of herself upon her return and in the months that had followed.

"It was more than that," Clay continued. "Her entire personality changed."

Not for the better, it was clear. And from what she knew of Clay, Tori had no doubt he must have become the father figure in his younger sisters' lives. For a twelve-year-old to carry such a burden was sad enough in itself. To know that the remaining parent had somehow let them down, as well, just shattered her heart.

"As if my father was the sole source of the good within her." He added, "And with her sudden unexpected transformation, she brought an immeasurable amount of ugliness into our lives. Everything turned dark." He exhaled a ragged breath. "I just don't see how Adria can forget any of that. Or pretend it never happened."

Tori's curiosity was nearly palpable. What did he mean by brought ugliness and darkness into their lives? Had it been deliberate? If so, how could a mother do that to her children? But he clearly wasn't going to elaborate any further. Not yet, anyway. And she wasn't going to ask him to. He would tell her what he felt comfortable divulging.

Without giving herself a chance to think, she laid her hand on his forearm and leaned into his side. His response was to wrap his arm around her shoulders.

Wordlessly, they walked further along the beach. Tori searched for words of comfort, anything to tell him how much she felt for the child he must have been. But none came to mind. She couldn't pretend to understand. Though she'd always felt that there was something in her life just out of range, her childhood had been happy and full of love. She wasn't equipped with the words of understanding she so badly wanted to offer him.

"That's your building, isn't it?" Clay asked after several moments, awkwardly dropping his arm from around her shoulders. The loss of warmth where his skin had touched hers was downright striking. Somehow, over the span of such a short time, she'd grown used to his touch. Heaven help her.

Tori nodded and let him turn her away from the water, toward the path that led to the residences. Within moments, they were standing in front of the glass doors of her building.

A battle warred within her chest. She wanted to learn more about him and the boy he had been, to ask him to come upstairs.

But was asking him to join her the smart thing to do? He'd almost kissed her twice already. They'd never actually been alone in a room together. Was she prepared for how far things could potentially go when it was just the two of them within four walls?

No matter what she was beginning to feel for Clay, she was here as a professional. He was technically her boss. She couldn't act like some hormonal teenager unable to rein in her desires or her emotions.

Not to mention, she was still a mess emotionally from the disastrous breakup with Drew. She wasn't exactly sharply tuned to the opposite sex, completely unskilled in the laws of attraction and the methods of flirtation. There was a distinct possibility she was misreading things between them.

It was all so wrong. But, somehow, nothing had ever felt more right.

Some sympathetic spirit above must have taken pity on her to help her make a decision; a low rumble of thunder grumbled through the air. Almost immediately, fat raindrops began falling from the sky.

Clay looked up at the layer of clouds that had

appeared above. "Great timing, I'd say. We got you here just in time."

"No so much for you. Aren't you on the other side of the resort?"

He chuckled. "It's okay. I won't melt."

Still, he grimaced as the rainfall intensified, accompanied by intermittent whipping winds.

"You could wait it out. I mean upstairs. With me." Why was she on the verge of stuttering incoherently? She was a grown, mature woman, for Pete's sake.

Clay merely quirked an eyebrow.

"Aren't tropical storms usually intense but quick? I'm sure it will stop in no time," she added. Tori wasn't certain who she was trying to convince, herself or Clay.

He tapped her nose playfully. "You sure you're not too tired? You were up at dawn baking cupcakes. And I'm guessing you have another early morning tomorrow."

"I'm sure. Besides, I find I'm still thirsty." She raised the wine bottle. "And we happen to have this perfectly good Sauvignon blanc."

He smiled at her, the tension in his face having completely dissipated since their walk on the beach.

"That's a tough invite to turn down."

"Then don't. Accept it. What do you say?"

"I say I'd be a fool to opt for making a mad

dash across the resort in pouring rain and hailing wind, when the other option is to share a bottle of wine with a pretty woman in a nice, comfortable hotel room."

The wise thing would have been to turn her down and just deal with the rain. He'd suffered worse things than a full drenching. Much worse.

But Tori's invitation proved too hard to resist. The way her eyes sparkled in the moonlight, how her hair curled gently around her face with the raindrops. One of her dress straps had fallen from her shoulder, exposing tanned golden skin his fingers itched to touch. She'd bunched up one side of the skirt of her dress, exposing a shapely leg.

It was all so beckoning.

A stronger man would have had the resolve to walk away, Clay thought as he followed her up the stone stairway and waited while she unlocked her door.

Light flooded the room as she flipped the switch and welcomed him inside.

Outside, the wind had grown harsher, driving the pounding rain almost horizontally now. "Thank you for sparing me from that," he said with gratitude, gesturing to the glass door of the balcony. Gentleman or not, he much pre-

ferred being indoors and relatively dry given
what mother nature had on display at the moment.

"It's the least I can do. You wouldn't even
be out this way if you hadn't walked me back.
Now, to find a corkscrew." She walked over to
the kitchenette where she began pulling open
random drawers. All of which appeared empty.

"Here. I'll look for it. I'm sure you want to
freshen up." After all, her dress had been par-
tially soaked before the rain had even started.

"I think I'll take you up on that. I do appear
to be somewhat damp."

As she headed to the adjacent bedroom, he
took over the search for the opener. Locating
it atop the mini fridge, he made quick work of
removing the cork and poured the wine into
two glasses.

Then he made his way to the sofa by the balcony and sat, watching the angry rain outside
the window. The weather didn't seem to have
calmed at all. Settling in the rather uncomfortable sofa, he waited for Tori to return.

And waited.

After about fifteen minutes, he walked over
to knock on her door. No answer.

"Tori, the wine is poured."

Nothing.

Should he be concerned? "Can I come in?"

There was some sort of mumbled reply. He pushed the door slightly ajar and poked his head inside. The image he encountered made him smile. Tori was out cold, sprawled on top of her bed. One sandal lay at the foot of the bed, the other dangled from her other foot. She hadn't even had a chance to take off the wet dress.

He knew she was wiped, but hadn't realized it would catch up with her so fast.

"So tired," she said through a muffled yawn when he reached the side of the bed.

"I know, sweetheart. I'm just going to lift you for a second to get you under the covers, okay?"

"'Kay."

He did the best he could, wishing he could unburden her of the uncomfortable dress but unable to find a reasonable way to do so. When she was adequately tucked in, he switched off the light and gently shut the door behind him.

The wine bottle sat mostly full, the glasses untouched. Clay had zero interest in having any of it by himself.

He settled on the couch—half slouched, half sitting on the hard, scratchy cushions. Tori wouldn't mind if he just waited out the storm here. Then he'd be on his way.

Only, when he next opened his eyes, the digital clock atop the television screen said two thirty. He jolted upright in the darkness. He'd been asleep on Tori's couch until past two in the morning.

Through sleep-dazed grogginess, Clay realized the creaking of a door was what had awakened him.

"Clay?"

He heard Tori's voice in the darkness. "I'm here. Hope I didn't startle you. Didn't mean to crash on your couch."

"And I didn't mean to fall asleep on you."

He chuckled. "You had a long day yesterday. I'm surprised you held out as long as you did."

"You can't be comfortable on that sofa."

He wasn't going to lie to her. His body felt like it'd been stretched atop a bed of sharp-edged boulders. His lower back was screaming at him.

"My fault for falling asleep. I'll just head out."

"It's almost dawn. You should just stay here."

"I don't think my back can handle it, sweetheart."

"I meant on the bed."

He wasn't sure how to respond to that, so he stayed silent, waiting for her to continue. The last thing either of them needed was a misinterpretation of intentions.

"You know, just to sleep," she finally added.

Clay pondered the unexpected offer. His back really did hurt. And it looked dark and wet outside. He'd be a glutton for punishment if he turned her down.

He silently followed her into the bedroom and lay on the mattress as far as he could from the other side without toppling over. He could hear her breathe, feel her warmth. So he didn't let himself move so much as a muscle.

A night-light illuminated the dresser across the room and he was amused to see the tattered stuffed rabbit that he'd noticed in her apartment back in Boston. So she traveled with it.

How utterly adorable.

"Who was it, then?" Tori asked, her voice thick with drowsiness. He wondered for a moment if she was talking in her sleep. Her next words clarified. "Your one invite to the wedding."

He had to chuckle. He'd forgotten even mentioning that to her earlier this evening.

"Did you see the short, gray-haired woman with all the silver bracelets on her arm? I believe she was wearing a purple top."

"Mmm-hmm. The one that looked like she could be everyone's grandmother."

That was the perfect way to describe Gladys

Thurman. "She's the one. She always wears at least a dozen silver bangles."

"Who is she?"

"Financial and operations director for Our New Start. It's a charity I run."

"You run a charity?"

"Figured I should. At least for a while. Since I founded it. Heard of it?"

She nodded. "Vaguely. You provide resources and youth centers for kids in homeless shelters throughout metro Boston."

"That's the one."

"You're quite an impressive man, Mr. Ramos."

Clay didn't know what to say to that, so he changed the subject. "Gladys is exactly what I'd imagine a charity representative would look li…ike." The last word came out on a rather large yawn.

Clay had a question of his own. "Tell me about this ex who didn't like you to dance," he found himself asking. He hadn't even realized he was going to bring up the subject.

He heard her sigh in the darkness. "It was more the way I danced. So he said, anyway. After he made a few too many comments, I became so self-conscious about it, I didn't even bother going anymore. Not even with girlfriends when he wasn't there." She took a deep breath. "It was just as well. He didn't really like hanging out with me when my girlfriends were around anyway."

The more she told him about this ex of hers, the more Clay was reminded of someone from his own life.

Someone who had nearly destroyed it.

He wanted to ask her about him, to find out more, but her breathing had evened to a slow and steady rhythm. If she wasn't already asleep, she certainly sounded close.

He'd learned so much about her tonight, but it would have to be enough for now. She was tired. And frankly, so was he. He found himself drifting off to sleep, as well.

All too soon, Tori's alarm went off and they both jolted upright and scrambled to get ready for the day. He did his best to freshen up before Tori jumped in the shower.

He was going to need a cold shower himself when he finally got back to his room. Lying next to her for hours, resisting the urge to reach out and touch her, had been nearly unbearable. Now, images of her under the spray of water, soaping up her skin…

He had to give his head a hard shake to clear the picture. By the time he stepped out of the building, the morning had turned bright and sunny. The chirping of birds rang through the air. He could hear the gentle crashing waves of the ocean in the distance.

A pair of joggers turned the corner along the pathway.

One of them glanced his way and did a double-take. She nudged her partner's arm until the man turned to look in his direction, as well.

Damn it.

The timing could not have been worse. His sister and Tom were early risers who liked to get a run in first thing in the morning.

The look of surprise on Gemma's face told him he'd have some explaining to do.

CHAPTER SIX

"You should probably know that my sister and her fiancé almost certainly believe that we've slept together."

Tori dropped the measuring cup full of sugar and swore at the mess that resulted on the previously pristine counter. A white cloud of powdered sugar hung in the air. She sneezed twice.

The batch of pie dough was ruined. She'd have to start all over again.

First things first, though.

"Come again?"

She couldn't have heard Clay correctly.

"Sorry. Didn't mean to startle you." He entered the kitchen and seemed to take stock of the mess he'd indirectly caused.

"What do you mean about your sister and Tom, exactly?"

He ducked his head with a sheepish set to his lips. "They saw me leaving your building."

She cupped a hand to her mouth. *Oh no.*

"You know, at dawn. After we'd been hanging out together the whole night before. Dancing, having cocktails," Clay added, as if she didn't know all that. As if she could have forgotten somehow. As if the whole evening and all that had happened afterward wasn't completely ingrained in her brain and would be for all time.

"Don't worry," he added, "I'll set them straight."

Somehow she didn't feel reassured.

This meant word would get out that she was sleeping with the boss. How utterly mortifying. Not that she had anything to be embarrassed about. She was a grown adult, after all. But the tabloid websites were constantly looking for juicy pieces about Clay and all it would take would be one wedding guest to be indiscreet once they returned Stateside.

Not the kind of attention Tori wanted as a professional business owner. Not to mention all the questions that would arise from friends and family. Questions she so didn't want to bother answering.

She would have to be so much more careful from now on. Should have never let her guard down in the first place.

But she'd already decided all that, hadn't she? This morning in the shower when she'd thought of how unaffected Clay had been even though they were merely inches apart atop the same bed. She'd been longing for his touch and he hadn't even so much as shifted near her.

Of course, he was solid and decent, the type of man who would never take advantage of circumstances. But he hadn't even showed the least bit of interest. While she'd been burning inside, yearning for him to touch her.

He could have asked.

Though, if he had, she had no earthly idea how she might have actually responded.

He gently took her by the upper arm and turned her to face him. "Hey, you're really upset about this, aren't you?"

"I'll be all right. Not upset so much as…"

"What?"

"I just feel embarrassed. I want Gemma and Tom to think of me as a professional." More than that, she wanted Clay's family to like her, to respect her.

And now they thought she'd slept with their brother after spending one evening with him at a party.

Heaven help her, she very well might have if he'd even showed the slightest interest. Clearly, she'd read more into what had been happening between them than reality merited.

"Don't be embarrassed. I'll talk to them first chance I get. Tell them nothing happened."

"Thanks. I guess that's all that can be done."

"I tried calling Gemma, but didn't get an answer. I'll track her down."

"I appreciate that. Do you think she may have mentioned it to anyone else?"

His expression told her she wasn't going to like the answer to that question. "Almost certainly. My other sister."

Adria, of course. It was going to be mortifying seeing either one of his sisters again.

Adria. Who would most likely then tell her husband. Who would then tell another guest, and so on and so on… It was like a mortifying game of phone tree.

Tori rubbed her forehead as a slight ache settled behind her eyes.

"I'm really sorry about this, Tori."

"Don't apologize. You didn't do anything wrong." Not even in the least. She should have simply retired to her room after the meal was over. What business had she had mingling with actual wedding guests? This was all her fault.

The only reason she was there was as an employee. How could she have forgotten that for even a moment? Simply because Gemma had been gracious enough to invite her to dinner.

"Thanks. I appreciate that. I'm sorry, too."

His eyes narrowed on her. "I was the one who got caught sneaking out of your hotel room. What in the world are you apologizing for?"

"If I've caused you any awkwardness with your sister or if I've embarrassed you." She knew she was overreacting—it wasn't as if she'd committed some kind of crime—but couldn't seem to help the sting of tears that suddenly burned behind her eyes. She couldn't imagine the way Clay's conversation with his sister might go.

He stepped closer to her. "Not this again. You said the same thing on the dance floor. It made no sense then, either." Clay raised her chin with his finger. "Hey. You did no such thing. It's just a silly misunderstanding and we'll set it straight."

"Thank you. I just don't like being the subject of gossip." Especially not with the type of crowd that was here at this wedding.

She'd been judged and found lacking often enough in the past.

Tori placed the tray of mini pastry crusts on the top rack of the oven and closed the door. She'd already whipped up the custard filling. The next step was to slice and glaze the tropical fruit that would serve as toppings on the tarts. But she couldn't bring herself to get started just yet. Usually, that was the piece of the fruit tart process she enjoyed the most. The sweet aroma of the fruit, the relaxing, repetitive motion of slicing. But today her heart wasn't in it. She needed a break.

This morning's conversation with Clay kept replaying over and over again in her mind. She wasn't looking forward to the next time she ran into the bride. Nor running into Clay again, for that matter.

She needed to vent, a shoulder to cry on. It would have to be a digital shoulder. Pulling out her cell phone, she clicked her sister's contact icon, not even caring about the time of day. Eloise was running back and forth from Sydney to Boston so often, Tori wasn't even sure where she might be at the moment. Her sister would have to forgive her for being awakened if that turned out to be the case.

"Tori!" Eloise immediately greeted, answering on the first ring. Simply hearing her voice had Tori's nerves soothing over. "I've been wondering when you'd call."

"Hey. Been meaning to. It's just been a little busy." And she'd been very preoccupied.

"So tell me, have you made your move on the hot architect yet?"

To her horror, Tori's bottom lip started to

quiver. She was just such a conflicted mess where Clay was concerned. And her sister's comforting, familiar voice had served to flush all of it to the surface.

Eloise picked up on her distress. "What is it? Tell me."

"Nothing. I'm fine." But her voice was so shaky, Tori hardly sounded convincing.

Eloise's voice grew firmer over the speaker. "Has that man done something to upset you? I can be on the next—"

"No! No, Eloise, he hasn't done a thing." That was part of the problem, wasn't it? Clay hadn't so much as kissed her, while she was a quivering mess of feelings whenever they were together. How could she even know if those feelings were entirely one-sided?

"Promise?" Eloise asked.

"Yes. Cross my heart." Tori made an X motion over her heart, which made no sense. It wasn't as if they could see each other.

"Then what is it, sis?"

Her twin's gentle prodding seemed to open the floodgates.

In a jumble of words, Tori blurted out everything that had happened, her embarrassment of the morning, and how confused she was about all of it. When she finished, she used the bottom of her apron to dab at her eyes.

Eloise had remained silent, patiently listening the whole time. Finally, she cleared her throat. "Wow. That's a lot."

Tori nodded. "Yeah, it is, huh?"

"So what are you thinking?"

"I don't think I know what to think. It's just… I haven't felt this way about anyone ever." And that was astounding considering she'd had the same boyfriend since tenth grade until they'd broken up a couple years ago. Or until she'd broken up with him, to be more accurate.

"I see," Eloise said after a long pause.

"And I don't know what good can possibly come of it. We're from two very different worlds. I only see him when he has need of a bakery."

"So you're thinking about what's going to happen in the long term."

"Doesn't everyone?"

"Not all the time. Sometimes people throw caution to the wind. They just act spontaneously."

"I know. But it's not how I'm wired."

"Maybe you need to be rewired—by a gifted and qualified electrician."

Tori guffawed at the ridiculous metaphor, which, of course had been Eloise's intent.

"Seriously, Tori," her sister added. "Look

how well things worked out for me and Josh when I finally decided to take a chance."

Tori tried not to scoff in dismissal. "It's hardly comparable, Eloise. You and Josh were the exception."

"I'd say your current scenario is pretty exceptional, as well. You're on a tropical island—a veritable paradise—far from home."

That was certainly the truth. "I suppose you might have a point."

Her sister chuckled softly. "Of course, I do. What better time to act a bit uncharacteristically?"

"Meaning?"

"Meaning don't look so deep into things. Don't overthink. Just see where things go and heed your heart about whether you'd like to follow or not."

Tori had to laugh at that. "Okay, you've moved from ridiculous metaphors to tired clichés. But I see your point. And I have to admit, you've given me a different perspective." She'd also managed to make her feel infinitely better.

"Hey, metaphors and clichés are what they are for a reason."

"I suppose that's true."

"So, will you try to throw some caution to the wind? And not be afraid to take a chance or two?"

Tori wasn't sure how to answer that. Not just yet. She decided to veer the subject back to Eloise's relationship instead. "So that's what you did with Josh, then? Took your chances?"

"Yes." The affection in her sister's voice for her new husband was clear as a bell, even over the phone. "You know I did. And he was absolutely worth it."

A smile spread over Tori's face. "Well, make sure you don't tell him that too often. Or he'll be even more insufferable," she joked.

Her sister chuckled. "I'll be sure."

Tori hung up after they chatted a few minutes longer, feeling much more lighthearted.

Without a doubt, her sister knew exactly what she spoke of on such matters. Eloise and Josh hadn't had the easiest time on their journey to happily-ever-after. Not that she and Clay were on any kind of romantic journey.

Was Eloise right? Was she just scared? She certainly had cause to be cautious, given the way things had gone with Drew—though Drew and Clay had absolutely nothing in common.

With a groan of frustration, Tori shook off the useless thoughts and went to replace her apron with a fresh one. Enough wasted time, she had to get started on that fruit. She couldn't avoid that part of the task any longer.

Like a lot of other things she wasn't going to be able to avoid.

"Are you certain you don't want to join us, Clay?" Gemma asked for the umpteenth time before boarding the van that would take the wedding party down to the retail area of the island. The planned excursion included a group shopping trip and outdoor beachside lunch. He had better things to do. He'd just wanted to catch his sister to explain about this morning before she and the others went on their touristy way.

He gave a mock shudder. "You know how much I loathe shopping."

Gemma laughed. "Okay. Guess we'll see you when we return." She turned back after stepping on the van's foot rail. "And apologies again for making assumptions about what I saw this morn—"

He held up a hand to stop her. "No need. I know how it must have looked."

He waved as the van drove away. Finally, some time to himself, and there was plenty of work to catch up on. But he was having difficulty making himself head back to his room to fire up the laptop.

Tori was avoiding him.

He'd sent her several texts that, so far, had gone unanswered.

He had wanted so badly to pull her into his arms this morning in the kitchen, to comfort her. He'd had no idea she would be quite so bothered by Gemma and Tom's incorrect assumptions about what had happened between the two of them last night.

Maybe even telling her that they'd seen him leaving her building hadn't been such a great idea. Tori would have been none the wiser. And he'd managed to set the record straight with his sister easy enough.

But he'd never been a big fan of secrets. Too late to ponder that score, anyway. Cat out of the bag and all that.

Now, he was just trying to determine what he was going to do about it. He didn't want there to be any kind of new weird dynamic between them simply because they'd spent one night together where nothing had ever happened.

A glance at his watch told him it was almost noon. She would be breaking for lunch at some point. Maybe they could grab a bite together.

At the least, he wanted to ask about the day's dessert she'd been working on. The nutty, fruity smell in the air had had his mouth watering this morning. Maybe she could use a taste tester. Funny how he'd never particularly had a sweet tooth until he'd met Tori.

Armed with his excuse, he made his way to the building that housed the kitchen.

He found her with her back to the kitchen door, standing at the counter, stirring the contents of a bowl the size of a small tub. She was holding a container of salt in one hand.

He approached her from behind and was about to announce himself, to ask if it was a good time for her to get away, when Tori suddenly threw a pinch of salt over her shoulder. The seasoning hit him square in the face.

Just to be funny, Clay faked a sneeze.

Startled, she turned with a hand to her chest. "Clay! Sorry about that."

"Beats being doused with iced coffee."

She blinked in confusion until the puzzle piece fell in to place. "Oh. Like that day at the bakery. Seems like years ago."

"Do you often toss salt around?"

"I just throw a pinch over my shoulder whenever I use it." Ducking her head sheepishly, she gave him a small smile. "Bit of a superstition. Doing so is supposed to be good luck."

"Till someone gets salt in their eye."

Her giggle had him lighting up inside.

"What does a pastry chef use salt for, anyway?" he asked.

"Just to bind all the flavors of the fruit together before I pour the glaze over."

"Huh. Fascinating."

"Is there something you wanted, Clay?"

"As a matter of fact, I thought maybe you'd need a taste tester."

She laughed. "You did, did you? I have no shortage of volunteers for that."

"Hmm. Shame. Also, I wanted to see if you'd be up for a break. Maybe to grab a bite?"

Her mouth tightened. "With you?"

The way she asked dealt something of a bruise to his ego. "That was the general idea, yes."

"But I thought you were heading into town with the others."

He shook his head. "Nope. Not my kind of excursion. I hate shopping."

"Surprising, when you have two younger sisters."

"That's precisely why. Been there, done that often enough already."

"Makes sense, I suppose. My brothers always complained when they were dragged out for school clothes."

"Speaking of siblings, I sat Gemma down after breakfast and told her exactly what happened last night between us. Or didn't happen, to be more accurate."

Her eyes widened. "You did? And she believed you?"

He shrugged. "Sure. Why wouldn't she? I have no reason to lie to her."

"True."

"She said it wouldn't have bothered her, by the way."

"Huh," she chided, "you might have led with that, Clay. Considering I've been fretting about it all morning."

"I left you several texts and a couple of voice mails." He watched as she lifted a pitcher-size measuring cup of glaze and slowly poured it into the bowl of fruit. "So, what do you say?"

"About Gemma not caring if we are…?"

"What? No. I was asking what you thought about getting some lunch."

"Oh. That. Well, I need to finish this up." She motioned to the bowl.

"I can wait."

Tori bit her bottom her lip at the lower corner and he had to make himself look away. She looked so utterly sexy when she did that.

"All right. I suppose I do need to eat at some point." As if on cue, he heard her stomach emit a low grumble.

"Again, you flatter me with your enthusiasm."

She took him by the shoulders and physically turned him the other way. "Right now, I have to get back to work. And you have to leave. Give me another hour or so."

"You got it." He let her give him a small shove toward the door. "I'm leaving."

"Yes, you are."

"You sure you don't need me to taste anything before I go?"

"Don't make me chase you out with the wooden spoon." Her warning fell flat thanks to the amused grin on her face.

Having lunch with Tori was a much better prospect than spending the day browsing trinkets and T-shirts. Even though he'd fully intended to utilize his free time on some much needed work—spending the afternoon being lazily unproductive was a foreign concept—he had no regrets about following this uncharacteristic whim in the least.

Then again, he was doing all sorts of uncharacteristic things on this trip. And the common denominator motivating those decisions appeared to be Tori Preston.

She drew him in like a magnet. The hours he spent alone while she'd been working seemed to drag on and on, and he often found himself counting the minutes until she'd be free.

But he wasn't smitten. Absolutely not. He

was just trying to break the monotony. Just because he was so drawn to the woman didn't mean his life would be altered in any way. Back in the States, he would return to long work hours and the occasional social outing to appease the clients who insisted on inviting him to their various functions.

That was the life he was meant to live. A solitary, peaceful one. He deserved it after what he'd been through.

And that life left no room for any kind of complicated relationship. Not even with someone like Tori.

Especially not with someone like Tori.

CHAPTER SEVEN

HE TOOK HER to a cabana beachside restaurant, one recommended by almost everyone on staff at the resort. The gentle lapping of waves by their table and the warmth of the afternoon sun set a soothing atmosphere and made for a picture-perfect lunch date. Clay felt his relaxation gradually grow to the point where the ever-present knot in his neck muscles slowly started to ease.

The menu wasn't vast but everything on it sounded delicious. Tori ordered fish tacos while he opted for spicy jerk chicken. By the time their food arrived, he'd kicked off his shoes and had leaned back casually in his chair. For her part, Tori looked fairly relaxed herself.

He was glad he'd cleared the air with Gemma about what had happened.

The waitress stopped by to refresh their waters. "I heard there was a wedding taking place on the resort," she said while she poured. "Would you two be the happy couple then?"

Tori paused in the act of lifting her taco to her lips, her cheeks reddening. "Uh, no."

"My sister is getting married. I'm here to walk her down the aisle," he explained.

"Oh, sorry," the young woman said with a bright smile. "Honest mistake. You two look like a lovely couple." Again, she'd made the wrong assumption. Why did that seem to keep happening to the two of them?

Tori's cheeks grew redder as she took a small bite of her taco. She looked so cute when she was blushing. "Mmm…" she moaned as she chewed.

Clay felt the now familiar tightening in his gut. How had he not realized before how sexy a woman who really appreciated food could be? Tori had grown up in the restaurant business; she baked for a living. Food was a center theme in her life. He was finding that ridiculously seductive and attractive about her.

One thing was certain—if he continued to watch her eat, he was going to be much too focused on her to enjoy his own lunch.

The burn on his tongue from his spicy dish was a welcome distraction.

"So tell me…" Tori began, dabbing at her mouth with a napkin. "If shopping is not your thing, what kind of outing would you have preferred?"

He smiled at the question. "I don't know if I want to tell you."

Her eyes lit with merriment and curiosity. "Well, now you have to."

"You'll laugh at me. Then tell me that it's something a little boy would want to do."

She leaned closer to him over the table. "I have two older brothers. I happen to know firsthand that all men are true little boys at heart."

She was right. Only, he hadn't felt like a little boy in a long time. There'd been no opportunity to act boyish since his father had died. And especially not since his mother had remarried after his father's death.

It was why he'd been compelled to found and nurture a charity specifically focused on underprivileged youth. Children who'd often not had the benefits and advantages of growing up in a stable and safe home. He could more than relate to those kids. His own family had been about as broken as could be if anyone had bothered to look under the surface of the façade.

He'd had to grow up quick. For his sisters' sake as well as his own. Maybe he'd tell Tori about it sometime… The thought took him by surprise. His past was not a subject he allowed himself to think about often, let alone discuss with others.

"I insist that you tell me," Tori ordered.

Clay did a double take. For a split second, he thought maybe she'd read his mind. But it occurred to him she was referring to the question she'd asked about his preferred outing.

"Fine then," he replied with feigned offense. "If you're going to get all bossy about it."

"Baby sisters have to be bossy sometimes."

That was certainly true, as he knew all too well. "Well, this island happens to be a maroon spot."

"A what? Like the color or something?"

She really was a delight. "No. Not the color. It was one of the islands that an unruly sailor who'd misbehaved was cast away on. It's said the famous pirate Killjoy Bob was deposited here after he tried a mutiny against his captain onboard his ship. They left him here to die with nothing but a half-empty bottle of rum."

She blinked at him, tilted her head. "Killjoy Bob?"

Clay could tell she was trying not to giggle. He crossed his arms in front of his chest. "Go ahead and laugh if you want. But there happens to be a whole pirate museum in downtown Nassau. Complete with a fake town and cruise tours aboard a pirate ship. You can even walk the plank if you'd like."

"Huh."

She leaned back in her chair and took another bite of her taco. "Again, I remind you that I have two brothers. Every time we went to the Cape, they made us do one of the many pirate tour attractions."

"Really?"

"Yep. In fact, they both mentor as Big Brothers. They take a group of kids every summer to the Cape and on one of those tours."

Her brothers sounded like fun, Clay mused, and like decent, honest men. Would they approve of him? he wondered. It was no secret he had a reputation as a hard-partying ladies' man who went through women like bar tabs. What brother would approve of someone like that for his baby sister?

Not that any of it made a whit of difference. He wouldn't be in Tori's life long enough for it to matter what her family believed of him. His spirits plummeting, he pushed the thoughts aside.

"Definitely," Tori answered. "Wait till I tell them I was on an authentic maroon island. They'll be so jealous." She threw her head back and laughed in a comically bad impression of some sort of movie villain.

"In that case, would you like to also tell them that you went to a real pirate museum?"

She set down her taco and focused an intense stare on his face. "Are you asking me?"

Looked like he was. "I was planning on going alone. No way I'm going to miss it. But I'd love the company."

The truth was, he hadn't really wanted to go by himself, not if there was a chance she might come with him. Despite what he'd just told her, he probably would have skipped it, hoped for another time.

Tori's answer brought an excited smile to his face. "Now, why would I turn down the chance to tease my brothers about how I was at a pirate town in the Bahamas?"

"Is that a yes?"

"You bet it is. Of course, I'll come with you."

"Then finish up. I'll call the concierge to arrange transportation."

Tori gave him a dramatic salute. "Aye, aye, matey."

Don't look so deep into things. Don't overthink. Just see where things go and heed your heart about whether you'd like to follow or not...

Her sister's words echoed through Tori's head as she rushed back to the kitchen to leave detailed instructions about how the tarts should be set out tonight at dinner. She'd be too busy to do it herself as she'd be playing the part of a lady pirate.

If it wasn't for Eloise and their phone conversation earlier this morning, Tori was certain she'd have turned Clay down. She would have thought of an excuse and spent the day in her hotel room reading or mindlessly watching TV. Instead, she was going to follow her sister's advice. And she wasn't kidding about rubbing it in her brothers' faces that she'd be experiencing an authentic pirate adventure. That was just an added bonus, like icing on the cake.

She was so deep in thought about the afternoon that awaited her, she almost missed the recognizable figure seated at one of the dining tables outside the food services building. Tori focused on what she could see of the woman's face to be certain of who it was.

There was no doubt. It was Adria, Clay's other sister. She was sitting by herself, her head bent, and she appeared to be clutching her middle.

Tori hesitated, deliberating what to do. Clay had ordered a car and was probably waiting for her right this minute. On the other hand,

Adria's entire demeanor looked as if she could use some kind of assistance.

There really was no decision to be made.

Tori approached the table and cleared her throat. "Hi, Adria."

Adria's head lifted ever so slowly. She just stared for a moment. Then her eyes seemed to clear with recognition.

"Tori, isn't it?" A shaky smile spread over her lips, her pallor the color of dewy damp grass on a New England morning. "You remember me then. You did the cake for my wedding, as well. Butter cream frosting. Marble sponge with seven tiers."

"A trophy," Tori supplied.

The woman's smile grew wider. "That's right. Somehow, you were able to craft it in the shape of a trophy."

"Your husband is a professional soccer player."

She nodded. "A striker for Madrid Royale. We didn't think you'd be able to do it. But you came through."

It had taken Tori weeks to try to figure it out. One of her most challenging creations. Most other cakes were…well, a piece of cake in comparison.

"You didn't go on the shopping excursion with the rest of the wedding group?" Tori asked. Why exactly was Adria here? And why did she look so unwell?

Adria visibly swallowed as if she'd just consumed something unsavory. "We came back early. I wasn't feeling well."

"Are you all right?"

"I'll be fine. Just the heat. And all the excitement. Enrique went to find me some crackers or something. Anything to help soothe a roiling stomach."

"Why don't we get you inside then?" Tori suggested. "Into the air-conditioning."

"You know, I think I'd like that." She pulled out her phone. "I'll just let Enrique know." After she fired off a text, they walked to the dining area of the main hall and Tori had her take a seat at the bar.

There were definitely some conclusions that could be drawn given the scenario before her. Adria still hadn't removed her left arm from where it rested on her stomach. She was clearly feeling nauseous. And she was holding her middle in a rather interesting way. Protectively.

Her years spent working in a restaurant, with a steady flow of female servers, Tori had encountered more than her fair share of pregnant colleagues. She'd be ready to bet money that Adria was expecting. Why she was keeping it a secret from everyone was a mystery however.

Tori was helping Adria get settled on a stool when her husband burst through the door. He was carrying Lilly in one arm and holding a grease-spotted paper bag in his other hand. Tall and lean, Enrique Maduro was the quintessential specimen of a Spanish heartthrob. Right now, however, he looked completely lost and panicked.

"I'm so sorry, *mi querida,*" he addressed his wife. "All I could find was some popcorn." He gave Tori a distracted nod of acknowledgment.

Adria visibly shuddered and turned a deeper shade of green. Her eyes grew shiny with unshed tears.

Greasy popcorn for a queasy stomach was far less than ideal, even under the best of circumstances.

To make matters worse, Lilly had her head draped on her father's shoulder and was hiccupping loudly. Her cheeks were wet and stained with streaks of tears. It appeared she'd just completed the mother lode of toddler temper tantrums. Tori couldn't decide which of the haggard trio before her she felt sorrier for. They all looked completely miserable.

None of this would do at all.

Tori reintroduced herself to Enrique and

gently took the bag of popcorn out of his hand. "Why don't you get Lilly back to your room? I'll make sure Adria gets something to eat that will calm her stomach."

One would think she'd just offered the man the key to eternal salvation. His look of relief was downright comical.

"Are you sure?" he asked.

Tori nodded. "Leave her to me."

He didn't argue. *"Gracias, señorita. Muchas gracias."*

With an affectionate kiss to the top of his wife's head, he bid Tori thanks once again, in English this time, then left.

Adria rested her head on the counter. "Just thinking about that popcorn makes me want to—"

Tori held her hand up to stop her from continuing. She could figure out the rest. It didn't help matters that the putrid aroma of burned grease still hovered in the air. She had to move quickly or Adria was sure to start to feel sicker. "There's a fresh baguette in the back that was baked just this morning. Loaded with a thick layer of sweet butter, it will make for a tasty, hearty toast. I'll also whip you up some scrambled eggs. Well done." Runny eggs would just make things worse. "The protein and the carbs mixed with a dose of fat should get you squared and feeling better in no time. And I'll pour you some ginger ale while you wait for the food."

It was Adria's turn to give her a grateful look. "You are a heaven-sent angel."

She shrugged. "Hardly. I just know when people need to be fed. I grew up working in my family's restaurant."

"Lucky for me you found me then."

Tori was spared the need to respond when Adria immediately followed her statement with a rather unexpected one. "So I hear you've been keeping my brother company these past couple of days."

Tori had to try hard not to betray any physical reaction to the mention of Clay. It wasn't easy. "We seem to be the only two people here unaccompanied."

Adria nodded. "I'm not sure why he came alone. But I'm glad he did."

It wouldn't do to read too much into that statement, tempting as it was to do so. "You are?"

"Yes. Some of the women he dates…" She let the sentence trail off.

Tori would ignore that. She didn't really want to think about the women Clay dated. Or who might be angry that she hadn't been invited to the wedding yet still awaited his return. That would be overanalyzing and she'd assured her twin that she was going to try to do as little of that as possible.

Easier said than done.

Pulling out a chilled can of soda from the industrial-size fridge, Tori set it in front of Adria after popping it open. "I'll get started on the food. It will just take a few minutes."

"You're very kind," she heard Adria say behind her as she pushed the kitchen door open.

When she returned with a full plate of hot food about ten minutes later, some of the natural color had returned to Adria's complexion. She was glad to see the ginger ale seemed to be doing the trick.

When Tori set the plate in front of her, Adria sighed. "So much better than greasy popcorn. Thank you."

"You're welcome."

"I feel strange eating when you're not having anything."

"I just finished lunch with—" She caught herself before his name dropped from her lips. Probably not a good idea to bring him up. But it was too late.

"My brother, I take it," Adria concluded with a knowing smile.

"Yes."

"It's good that you kept him company while

the rest of us were out. He wanted to do something completely different as an excursion."

And not one of them had even entertained the idea.

"He told me," Tori said. "Pirate town."

Adria smiled around a forkful of food. "That's right. He's always loved pirates. Since he was a little boy."

"Then perhaps someone should have accommodated that one small interest of his?" Tori wanted to suck the words back as soon as she'd said them. None of this was really any of her concern. She certainly had no business second-guessing the bride's wishes let alone the wedding party's. Plus, in all fairness, Adria and Enrique had more pressing matters to deal with.

"I'm sorry, I shouldn't have said that."

Adria set her fork down. "No. You have every right to say what you think. Ironic that Clay finally has someone defending him for a change." Her voice trembled slightly as she spoke.

"I don't understand."

She gave her head a shake, as if she'd been the one to say too much this time. "Never mind. It's not important right now. And you happen to be right. We owe Clay a debt of gratitude that neither Gemma nor I will ever be able to repay. A debt that has nothing to do with him financially taking care of us. Or paying for elaborate weddings, by the way. We could have at least extended the courtesy of indulging him with something he wanted to do."

Tori waited for her to elaborate but it was as if Adria had read her mind. "You'll have to ask him about it yourself."

She could try. Something told her that asking Clay anything about his past would be fruitless, however. Plus, the whole conversation was starting to make her feel uncomfortable.

"You'll have to excuse me," she told Adria, perhaps a little too abruptly. "I have to go leave some instructions to the staff about tonight's dessert."

Adria was gone when Tori returned. She'd left her a little note on a napkin.

Feeling much better. Thank you for your kindness.

I'm guessing you've figured out my little secret. Please be discreet and help me to keep it a while longer.

She'd included a cell phone number. *Curiouser and curiouser,* Tori thought as she folded the napkin and placed it in her pocket. It seemed the more she learned about Clay, the more mysterious he became.

What was taking her so long?

Clay stood leaning against the wall by the entrance of the resort trying not to count down the minutes until Tori showed up. Had they miscommunicated the meeting spot? That didn't seem likely. The plan had been pretty clear.

Had she changed her mind?

It would be unlike Tori to just have a sudden change of heart like that. And even more unlike her to not even let him know. Maybe she'd lost the connection on her cell phone.

He was beginning to panic when he finally saw her through the glass doors. A surge of relief flooded his chest. He'd been worried about her.

And worried that she might have decided to blow him off.

After all, it was rather silly when he thought about it. For a grown man to be excited about visiting a fake pirate town. Tori was probably just being polite, too embarrassed for him to up-front turn him down.

Nevertheless, now she was here and he was glad for it.

So he had no idea why he'd snapped at her

when she reached him. "I was beginning to think I'd only imagined that you'd agreed to come."

She didn't take the bait. In fact, she looked rather distracted. "Sorry, I ran into someone."

"You couldn't stop chatting with this someone long enough to let me know?"

Her eyebrows drew together as she squinted at him in the sunlight. "My phone wasn't readily available. Are we going to go or not?"

Great. Now they were both annoyed. Should make for an enjoyable day then, with the two of them snapping at each other for no real reason. He was going to suggest that maybe they forget the whole thing but Tori was already walking down the wooden pathway that led to the catamaran.

Uttering a curse under his breath, he followed her.

By the time they arrived at the main island and reached the awaiting car, the tension between them had only grown thicker.

Their driver wordlessly started the engine and drove down the long driveway before pulling out onto the main road. An awkward silence ensued with only the vehicle's navigation system doing any talking.

They drove that way with neither saying a word for about seven minutes before Clay couldn't stand it any longer. "Look, I'm sorry if I sounded short with you back there. I was worried, that's all."

She tilted her head. "Thank you for the apology," she said simply, somewhat surprising him. Most of the women he dated prolonged his attempts at atonement. He'd been fully expecting to have to border on groveling to break the tension between them.

Then she surprised him even further with her next words. "And I'm sorry for making you worry," she added. "I should have found a way to let you know I was running late. It was unfair to you."

Her words echoed in his head. For the life of him, he couldn't remember receiving a genuine apology from someone in his lifetime. He was always expected to be the strong one. The rock.

Heaven knew, the one person on earth who was supposed to care for him and protect him had failed miserably. It would never occur to his mother to apologize for any of it. On the contrary, she refused to even acknowledge the neglect, would never take any responsibility for any wrongdoing.

"Apology accepted," he mumbled. But Tori had already turned to stare out her window at the passing scenery, unaware of the impact her words had delivered.

Finally, he eyed the specter of a large make-shift pirate's ship in the distance, complete with the skull and crossbone flags and willowy sails at full mast.

"Oh my God," Tori exclaimed next to him with clear glee.

"Impressive, huh?"

"It's even better than I had thought."

She really was excited to be here. Maybe even more than he was. He should have never doubted her.

The first exhibit took Tori's breath away, though to call it an exhibit was a discredit. They stepped into a moonlit night in the year 1716 on what appeared to be an authentic era dock. The sounds of lapping waves and rough-housing pirates in the distance added to the ambience. She could even smell the salty, fishy aroma of the ocean.

She couldn't help her squeal of delight. "I feel like Blackbeard is going to come walking out from behind that ship any second."

"With a yo-ho-ho and a bottle of rum."

She couldn't tell which one of them looked more entranced with the place. Oh yeah, her brothers were going to hear all about this museum.

Tori hadn't realized she'd said the last bit

out loud. "You're gonna rub it in their faces huh?" Clay teased. "That you got to see this and they didn't?"

"Absolutely. Josh, too. He'll also be green with envy. Though I don't dare call it a museum or they'll stop listening."

Clay laughed as they walked further along the makeshift quayside in the shadow of a frigate. A drunken "pirate" lay sprawled on the ground in front of the pub. A loud argument could be heard from inside in clear pirate brogue.

"Want to board the ship?" Clay asked.

"You need to ask?"

They walked up the wooden ramp, which creaked loudly with each step. She could have sworn she felt the frigate rock as if it was really navigating ocean swells. An open treasure chest sat at the top of the ramp and there was a large map of the Bahamas on the wall.

It took a full hour to explore all of the attractions on the pirate ship alone. By the time they walked out of the museum, the afternoon had grown dark. Tori wore a felt pirate's tricorn adorned with a skull and crossbones in the front while Clay brandished an aluminum cutlass.

"I could use a drink," Clay announced, pointing to the pub next door.

"I'll find a table if you go to the bar."

He gave her a pirate's salute. "Anything for the fine young lady." His accent needed work.

"Why, thank you, guv'nor." Okay, so her accent wasn't all that much better.

Tori pulled her phone out as soon as she sat to take notes about everything they'd just experienced. She didn't want to miss any details when she told the three wannabe swashbucklers back home about any of this.

She had a full screen written by the time Clay arrived with two of the day's rum cocktail specials.

"That was a tour I'll never forget." And she had Clay to thank for it. Spending time on a makeshift pirate ship and walking through a replica eighteenth-century town was not something that would have even occurred to her.

"Same. Can't wait to do it again."

To her surprise, he reached across the table and took her hand in his. "Thanks for coming, Tori. Really."

An electric current ran up her arm and down her spine from the contact point. She would never get used to the way her body reacted whenever this man touched her.

She tried for a nonchalant shrug. "Sure. What are friends for?"

"Is that what we are, then?" he asked,

his voice thick with heat and promise. "Just friends?"

He dropped her hand and pulled away before she could even think of a way to answer.

Tori took a sip of her drink, suddenly warm from the inside out. Though it tasted heavenly—a perfect combination of tart and fruity—the cocktail didn't do much to cool her down.

"So who'd you run into?" Clay was asking.

It took a moment to process what he meant.

"Before we left the resort," he added.

"Your sister, actually."

His eyebrows shot up. "How was Gemma back so fast? That shopping trip was supposed to take all day."

"Not Gemma. Adria."

A shadow crossed his face. "Oh. I'm guessing Enrique grew impatient and wanted to come back early. He enjoys such outings even less than I do."

Tori stayed silent, letting him run with his conclusion about Adria's early return. Trying to correct him could lead to a verbal land mine she didn't want to try to navigate. A slip-up would be all too easy.

"I haven't spoken to her in a few days," he said on a deep sigh. "Been meaning to rectify that. Just don't want to start an argument."

Tori knew she had to tread carefully. The last thing she wanted was to betray Adria's trust. Another woman's secret was not hers to tell, especially not one on that level of importance. Though maybe this rift between siblings could be faster healed if Clay knew. Still, it was not her place to decide.

"I would say it's worth a try. Risk of argument notwithstanding. Maybe you two just need an open and honest sit-down."

"And I should make the first move?"

She leaned further toward him. "Someone has to."

He rubbed his eyes and took a deep swallow of his drink. "I know you're right. Just putting it off."

He'd mentioned their mother had had something to do with whatever they were butting heads about. "I'm sure you both have valid viewpoints. Might be worth simply weighing those against each other."

He scoffed. "If only it were that simple. For some reason, Adria suddenly decided she'd like to contact our estranged mother. I can't begin to imagine why."

What exactly was the story there? The mother had never been involved in the previous wedding. And the woman certainly wasn't in attendance at this one.

"Adria found her on some social media site," Clay continued. "They've been messaging or whatever the kids call it."

"I see." Tori was beginning to see, indeed. She could think of more than one reason a woman experiencing an exhausting pregnancy might want to seek the comfort of a mother, estranged or not. Adria probably felt vulnerable and in need of nurturing. As considerate as Clay was as a brother, he wasn't exactly the nurturing type. And while Gemma and Adria seemed close, Gemma was on the brink of a whole new chapter in her own life. Which would no doubt mean less support and sisterly affection.

Though, judging by Clay's attitude, their mother clearly hadn't been all that loving.

"Hard to believe she even wanted to send her a last-minute invite to the wedding," Clay snapped through gritted teeth.

"And you refused."

He thrust his hand through his hair in frustration. "Not exactly. But something close to that."

"Oh?"

"I told her that if that woman attended, I certainly would not."

"Oh, Clay."

"I know it sounds extreme. Unreasonable.

But, trust me, I have my reasons. That woman has no business reentering our lives. Not for any reason."

Tori searched his face, silently willing him to continue. To just get it all out in the open, to maybe purge himself of the burden of it once and for all.

He finally began after several tense moments. "She remarried within a year after my father died," he told her. "And my stepfather was not a very nice man."

It was her turn to reach for him.

"In fact, he was skillfully cruel," Clay added.

"Your mother didn't stop it in time."

He grunted in disgust. "Worse. She pretended it wasn't even happening."

Clay's mouth had gone dry. Surprisingly, he looked down to find he'd already polished off his drink. Tori held firmly to his hand, her comfort and warmth spreading through him, right to his core.

Her eyes had grown shiny. But he didn't see any pity in their depths. That, he wouldn't have been able to bear. No, the only emotion he could sense was pure empathy.

"Tell me," she said on a shaky whisper.

The memories came roaring back like a tsunami of shame and anger. And hurt. Then the words just started to pour out.

"He loved to remind me that I was weak. I was never the sort of son he would have wanted."

"Weak? You were a child." Tori's voice shook with outrage on his behalf.

"A child who always had his head in a book. Or was sketching a picture or a design of some sort."

"And now you're a famous, accomplished architect. You must have had talent even at such a young age."

"He didn't see it as talent. He saw it as dreamy and worthless. At least I was able to keep him away from Gemma and Adria. That was all that mattered. The more he focused on what a disappointment I was, the less he was interested in the two of them."

She squeezed his hand. "You turned yourself into bait. To protect your sisters."

He shrugged. "What choice did I have? I could handle him. They wouldn't have been able to. He could be vicious."

"He was physical, wasn't he?"

"Yeah, but he was sneaky about it."

"Sneaky?"

"Yeah. A baseball would get misthrown and hit me in the chest. Somehow I wouldn't see his feet while running and trip over them. Things like that."

Now that he was saying the words out loud, the confusion and anger of those years threatened to bubble to the surface. Somehow focusing on Tori's face served as a buffer. "He just said it was proof I was not athletic and that my clumsiness was the reason any of it was happening."

"As though it was all your fault."

"Exactly. And my mom believed him. Because it was easier for her."

"I'm so sorry you had to go through that. No child deserves that."

He sneered. "If my mother thought so, she didn't bother to say it. Or do anything about it."

"You have every right not to want to forgive her."

Forgiveness had never even crossed his mind, not since he'd walked out of his mother's house for the final time years ago, taking both his sisters with him.

Why Adria felt the need to revisit any of the past was beyond his comprehension. She hadn't seemed to be able to give him any kind of answer when he'd asked. Yet somehow she was looking to open a sealed door that would let that past horror gush back into their lives. For no good reason that he could see.

Clay suddenly felt a heavy weariness settle over him. He hated that he was fighting with his sister. But her motives just didn't make any sense.

"Is that why you set up a charity for children?" Tori asked him now.

He shrugged. "I suppose it had a lot to do with it. My only escape growing up was a local teen center. It ran solely on donations and volunteers. The only peace I had was when I escaped there for a game of basketball or to just hang out. I guess I wanted to pay it forward."

"That was very noble, Clay. I hope you see that."

"I don't know about that." He stared at his empty glass. "Being able to do something for those kids benefits me as much as it benefits them."

Her eyes softened even as her grip on his hand tightened. "That says a lot about you. Tells me all I need to know about your character."

Clay wasn't sure what that meant. How could he explain to Tori that helping those kids helped him to recapture some of the innocence he'd abruptly lost when he'd had to grow so suddenly after his father's death.

Not that he needed to explain it. And he certainly didn't need to unburden himself this way to her. "We don't need to talk about any of this. It's all in the past. What's done is done." He took his arm away, perhaps a little too forcefully. Tori slowly placed her hand back at her side.

"I could use another drink." Standing on shaky legs, Clay took his time walking over to the bar. He needed a moment, without Tori watching him with those kind, sympathetic eyes. Part of him felt rather relieved that she knew about that part of his life now. Another part felt shaky and vulnerable.

Is that what love is, then?

Whoa. What?

Clay froze in place. How had that word even come up? He really was a mess, throwing such loaded words around even silently. Yes, he and Tori appeared to be compatible in any number of ways. And clearly there was some sort of spark between them, a current of electricity. There was just so much about her he liked and admired. Her kindness. Her dedication when it came to her craft. The way her smile brightened a darkness within him that he'd never thought would see light.

But none of that meant love. He'd seen what love could be when his father was still alive. His parents had truly been happy together.

Clay had also seen what love was not. He'd

seen how losing the man she'd adored had broken all that was decent within his mother. What his stepfather and she had shared was nothing more than an attachment to each other, a codependency that had led his sole remaining parent to neglect and betray the very same people she was supposed to cherish and protect.

Why would Clay risk leaving himself open to such vulnerability? Especially after what he'd overcome.

He and Tori weren't even dating, for Pete's sake. They'd just been spending time together for a few days, not even that long.

Must have been something in that drink. He was going to switch to soda.

It was completely dark by the time they made it back to the resort and Clay walked her to her room.

Tori's heart still felt heavy thinking about their conversation at the bar. The things about his past that he'd confided in her would stay with Tori for the rest of her life. People could be so cruel. And those who were meant to protect the most vulnerable so often couldn't be bothered to do the right thing.

How little she'd known about him all this time. To think, she'd found him attractive before. To know now all that he'd overcome, and just how far he'd made it in life despite such punishing odds, added admiration to the myriad feelings she felt for Clay Ramos.

Including longing.

She couldn't deny it any longer. She yearned for him, wanted him with every cell in her body, down to her bones.

So what was she going to do about it?

"Thanks again for being my pirate playdate," he said with a smile that seemed less than heartfelt. No wonder. Their lighthearted afternoon had certainly grown heavy into the evening.

"You're welcome." She held up the silly pirate's hat. "Thank you for my souvenir."

"You're welcome. Have a good night." He saluted her with the fake cutlass before landing a soft peck on her cheek.

Tori's heart pounded in her chest as he made to leave. He'd taken one step before she found her tongue. "Wait!" She hadn't meant for her voice to sound quite so urgent.

Clay turned, giving her an inquisitive look. "Something wrong?"

No. Yes. How was she going to articulate what she wanted? She had no experience with this. With Drew, he'd always been very clear about what he'd been after. Her desires and needs had always been afterthoughts.

She wasn't used to asking for what she wanted.

The truth was, she'd felt a kindred spirit when Clay had told her about his stepfather. In so many ways, she could relate to how he'd been mistreated by the bullying adult his mother had brought into their lives.

Unlike her, however, Clay hadn't chosen his tormentor. And he'd found a way to channel his turmoil into something productive and charitable. He'd found a way to help others, whereas Tori had barely been able to help herself.

Well, maybe this would be step one of that process.

"I'd like it if you would come in. Very much," she managed to blurt out.

Heat flooded his eyes and the muscle in his jaw clenched. "There's no storm tonight, sweetheart."

Aside from the proverbial storm raging within her. "I know. And I know what I'm asking."

"I'm not certain you do. Or if you've thought it through all the way."

Her heart plummeted to her toes. If this was his way of telling her he'd rather not be with her, she didn't think she would ever recover.

But she wasn't about to walk anything back. Much too late for that.

Her expression must have given away her thoughts.

"You can't think I don't want you," he said on a low growl. "You have to know better than that."

Relief and joy blended into a potpourri of emotion through her core. Her body was humming, her desire ratcheting up several notches at hearing that he did indeed want her, too. "Then what are we going to do about it, Clay?" The answer was oh so obvious as far as she was concerned.

"If this is some kind of pity—"

She physically clasped her hand over his mouth. "Please stop right there. Before you say something we're both going to end up regretting."

He gently pulled her hand from his lips. "I'm sorry. It's just been an intense couple of hours. I don't want there to be any misunderstandings between us."

"There won't be. I understand what I'm asking for."

He gently trailed a finger down her cheek then tucked a loose strand of her hair in place behind her hear. "Are you sure, Tori? Because I'm trying to be really up-front here. I can't be someone I'm not. And I can't give something I don't have to give."

"Then I'll take whatever you can give." She made sure to emphasize the last two words.

Dear heavens, who was this daring, unapologetic woman so blatantly stating what she was after? Tori didn't think she'd ever been so bold in the past, or could ever be so bold again.

And then she couldn't think at all. Clay's hand moved with lightning speed to grasp the back of her neck under her hair. He pulled her to him and took her mouth with his in a way that could only be described as savage. Demanding. Punishing. In all the best ways. She groaned under his mouth, let her hands roam across his chest and along his shoulders. Beneath his shirt, his skin felt like fire under her fingers. Her mind simply screamed for more.

He was pushing the door open behind her, half carrying her inside, their lips still fused together.

They didn't make it past the sofa until several hours later.

CHAPTER EIGHT

TORI DIDN'T HAVE to open her eyes to know that the bed was empty. She could feel his absence. Had he just up and left? It seemed implausible, after the night they'd shared, that he wouldn't so much as bid her good-bye before just taking off.

Memories flushed through her mind and she felt her cheeks burn. Clay had been arduous yet gentle. Demanding yet generous. Her body still tingled in response.

But now he was gone.

Forcing one eye open, she glanced around the room. Though his pants were nowhere to be seen, his shirt still lay where he'd haphazardly tossed it on the floor last night.

So he was here somewhere still, unless he'd dashed shirtless across the resort to his own room. Highly unlikely. Maybe he was getting a drink of water or something. She could use some herself. Embarrassingly enough, she found herself giggling. Maybe they could take up where they'd left off.

The sound of the balcony door opening then shutting again solved the mystery. He'd simply been out for some air.

He appeared in the doorway a moment later. "What's got you so amused this bright and early in the morning?"

"Is it that obvious?"

"Very."

"I was just remembering," she said with a coyness that surprised her. Even her voice sounded unfamiliar to her own ears.

He reached for her stuffed rabbit where it sat on the TV stand. "This thing's been staring at me. Rather accusingly, I might add. As if I took his spot last night."

Tori laughed. "I've had that for as long as I can remember."

He studied the worn and tattered outer material. The thing had been patched up more times than the scarecrow in that children's story. "I can tell. It's clearly seen better days. I saw it in your apartment back in Boston. So you travel with it, too, huh?"

She nodded. "It's the only thing I have of my biological mother. She gave Eloise and me identical stuffed rabbits before we were adopted out."

"Ah, so it's sentimental."

"Very." How odd that they were speaking about her stuffed rabbit when all she wanted to discuss was what they'd shared last night. Wasn't he feeling the slightest bit affected?

He walked over to the bed and handed her the toy, then gave her a tender peck on the cheek. Chaste. Innocent. Completely different than the way he'd kissed her last night.

It took all she had not to grab his arm and pull him down onto the mattress. Something told her it wouldn't be a good idea. That the reaction she'd receive wouldn't be entirely what she hoped for.

She propped her pillow and sat straight instead, the stuffed rabbit clutched snugly to her chest. "Were you just getting some air out there? On the balcony?"

"Actually I was just waiting for Gemma and Tom to come by on their morning run. We don't want a repeat of the last time I left your place in the morning. This time I don't think she'd quite believe it if I tried to tell her that nothing happened between us." With that, he picked his shirt up and began putting it on.

Tori reflexively tugged the sheet up higher over her breasts, suddenly feeling exposed.

"I've got something of a busy day," he told her, buttoning up.

Family events. And she certainly wasn't family. In fact, she wouldn't even know what to call herself as it pertained to Clay. She certainly wasn't his girlfriend.

She baked cakes for him.

"But I'll call you later," he said. "Maybe come by if you're up for it. No pressure, of course."

She could only nod, her tongue didn't seem to want to work. Just as well. Nothing she could have said would fit the current scenario.

He didn't want to be seen leaving her room. Plus, he wasn't even interested in seeing her again until later tonight. Why was she so unprepared for this? How had she not seen it coming? There was no excuse for such naïveté. Clay had felt vulnerable yesterday after their heartfelt conversation in the pub. He'd taken her up on her offer of a night of comfort. That's all their intimacy amounted to. Nothing more.

He couldn't have been more clear last night. And he couldn't be clearer now. To him, this was all nothing more than a meaningless fling.

Well, if that thought left a lump of disappointment lodged in her throat, she had no one but herself to blame.

He had been up-front with her, after all.

His sister looked beat.

Clay supposed that wasn't surprising given

that she was the mom of a very energetic toddler. Still, Adria appeared as if she wanted to go to sleep right there on her lounge chair by the pool.

By contrast, her daughter didn't seem even remotely interested in napping. In fact, Lilly looked to be on the verge of a toddler tantrum. Growing impatient with having sunblock applied, she kept trying to slip out of her mother's arms.

He walked over to where they sat and crouched to his niece's level. "Hey, squirt, what seems to be the matter here?"

"No hat!" she yelled, and tried to yank her sunbonnet off her head. Apparently, her headwear was an issue as well as the dreaded sunscreen lotion.

"She's been in a mood all morning," Adria told him. "She's got me at my wit's end."

"Want Daddy!" Lilly demanded.

Uh-oh, Lilly's voice had risen a notch. The tantrum was looking inevitable.

"Daddy's on an important phone call, love," Adria told her daughter in a most soothing and calming voice. "Contract negotiations," she added for Clay's benefit.

He'd been out walking the resort to get some air, anything to try to clear his head, when Lilly's voice had carried across the patio. Not that his walk had been doing him any good anyway.

The way he'd left things with Tori this morning wasn't sitting well with him. She'd refused to meet his eyes as he'd walked out the door, had just clutched her toy rabbit tightly in her arms.

She'd looked so vulnerable, so damn hurt, that he'd almost turned around and crawled back under the covers with her. He'd so badly wanted to. But in the end, doing so would have only served as a temporary salve. Eventually, he would have to leave her bed, and leave her room. Just as, eventually, he would have to walk out of her life. For he would never be able to fit in to it. Tori's life was full of the love of a strong family and the challenge of a successful business. She didn't have room in it for a man like him. A man with a past that haunted him.

"Wanna swim!" Lilly shouted, breaking into his thoughts. She thrust a pudgy hand toward the pool "Wid Daddy."

Clay lifted the little girl in his arms and held her close to his face, her feet dangling playfully. His efforts got him a few solid kicks to the stomach. "Listen, squirt, your momma says Daddy's busy. How about if I take you in the pool instead?"

Her angry grimace immediately transformed

into a wide grin. She clasped her hands on his cheeks. Clay decided he'd take that as a yes.

"Oh, Clay. Would you really do that?" Adria asked in a hopeful voice. "I could really use a break here."

He set his niece down on the concrete patio and fixed her bonnet.

"Sure. I'm not really doing anything right now."

As far as olive branches went, he figured it was a start. After the conversation at the pub yesterday, Tori's words about Adria in particular had rumbled around in his head. Tori was right. He should have probably listened better when Adria had first raised the subject of their mother. He was a mature, professional adult. The mere mention of his mother shouldn't have him seeing red and refusing to even hear his sister out. Ultimately, nothing Adria could say would ever change his mind about the family matriarch, but listening was free.

Tori. So much for clearing his head. Thoughts of her had nagged at him all morning. He couldn't seem to get her out of his mind. Nor what they'd shared last night.

He had to come to terms with what had happened between them. He couldn't recall the last time a woman had gotten so deep under his skin.

"And where did you just drift off to?" Adria asked, pulling him back to the present.

"Just planning all the water games this little one and I are about the play," he lied. "Why don't you lay back and close your eyes for a bit?" She really did look tired. A bout of brotherly sympathy and concern settled in his chest.

They'd been through a lot together, the three of them. He couldn't ever forget that. He'd always feel responsible for her and Gemma on some deep level, no matter how old they got. Ingrained habits were hard to break.

His two sisters were the only family he really had. Plus the little one currently tugging at his hand, trying to drag him to the water. But she was a fairly new addition to the mix. And he would have yet another brother-in-law soon. Thankfully, they were both good men. But Clay wasn't at the point yet where he viewed either one as family. More like good friends or poker buddies, perhaps.

He was happy his sisters had found love and wanted to marry. He really was. The chances of him doing the same were slim to none. He'd already spent years feeling responsible for others, had finally reached a point in his life where he could focus on himself and his career goals.

It would be selfish of him to pull anyone

else into his orbit when he had so little to offer. That's why he'd been absolutely straight with Tori last night. He could only hope she'd understood like she said she did.

A small hand smacked him on his knee. "Swim!"

Man, females could be so impatient.

Clay shrugged off his shirt, glad he'd thrown on nylon sports shorts this morning. He walked his niece to the edge of the pool and helped her navigate the steps.

Lilly held her arms up and pumped her legs.

"You want to be tossed, huh?"

"Up!"

And so began a marathon game of toss and catch until his upper arms started to ache. At least it looked like his sister was getting some R and R.

Tori's breath caught when she saw him.

Some unexplainable instinct had made her take the long way to her room after finishing the day's baking. She'd figured she'd take the scenic route that ran along the path leading to the infinity pool that served as the central landmark of the resort.

Clearly, said instinct wasn't of the self-preserving variety.

She couldn't help but stand and stare at the

sight of Clay in the pool. Even the risk of being caught wasn't enough to make her turn around. She was mesmerized by the image he posed.

There he was, shirtless and tanned, playing with his niece. Something about seeing Clay swimming with the little girl, watching how affectionate and playful he was with her, had Tori's heart pounding in her chest. Pictures from the previous night flooded her mind. Her cheeks started to flame as a welcome warmth curled through her midsection.

Finally, she tore her gaze away and forced her jaw closed. It wasn't easy.

She'd almost made her getaway sight unseen when a familiar female voice called out her name. "Tori. Is that you?"

Clay's head snapped in her direction and a bolt of electricity shook her entire body when their eyes met. He almost missed catching his niece as she came down from the last toss, but managed to snatch her just in time. Tori uttered a mild curse. If she'd only stepped away a second sooner.

Maybe she could pretend she hadn't heard her name. But that was fruitless. Clay had locked eyes with her. In fact, he was staring at her now.

Adria sat up in her lounger and patted the

chair next to her. "Come sit with us a bit. I just ordered a pitcher of lemonade."

Not exactly having a choice, Tori slowly made her way over.

"Again, Unca' Cway." Lilly's joyous shout echoed through the air.

"How are you feeling?" Tori asked, keeping her voice low, not that she could have been heard over toddler laughter and splashing water.

"More and more tired every day."

"Sorry to hear that. How about the nausea?"

"That can be kept at bay as long as I stay out of the heat." She pointed to the beach umbrella above her. "And if I make sure to eat."

"Is there anything I can bake for you?" Tori didn't envy the woman. A sweltering tropical island could only be so much fun while expecting. "Any cravings yet?"

Adria rested her hand on her middle. "Too many to mention, unfortunately."

"Please let me know if there's anything I can prepare for you."

Adria tilted her head, examining her. "Thank you. You really are a kind soul, aren't you?"

Tori shrugged. "I just happen to have an entire kitchen at my disposal."

Adria patted her knee. "I just may take you up on that. With Lilly, I only wanted savory dishes." She gave her belly a small affectionate rub. Tori didn't think Adria was even conscious of how often she touched her middle. "This one seems to have burdened me with a raving sweet tooth."

"It's a good thing your brother hired a baker then, I guess."

The woman chuckled melodically. "Good thing, indeed."

Adria was easy to talk to. Despite the disconcerting fact that Clay was so close and half undressed, chatting with his sister was starting to put Tori at ease. Heaven knew she could use it.

Judging by her next statement, Adria seemed to feel the same way. "You know, it's nice to be able to finally talk to somebody about all this. Besides Enrique."

"It must be hard to keep it completely close to your chest."

Adria shaded her eyes with the back of her hand. "Harder than I would have thought, to be honest." She sighed deeply. "You're wondering why I won't tell anyone."

The question had crossed her mind.

"It's simple, really," Adria continued. "This is Gemma's time. I don't want anything overshadowing her special day."

It was such a selfless motive. Tori's impression of the woman went up several pegs from an already pretty esteemed level. But her reasoning still didn't explain why she hadn't told those closest to her. Including her brother. Clay seemed like the type who could hold a secret.

"Do you mind if I'm honest about something else?" Adria asked.

"Of course. Please go ahead."

"I have to say, I had my suspicions, but there's really no doubt watching the two of you up close."

Tori gave her head a shake. "I don't understand."

"You've really got it bad." She motioned toward her brother. "The way you keep looking at him but pretend that you're not."

Tori felt heat rush into her face. "Oh no. It's not like that." Had Clay noticed her staring at him, too? She probably looked like a love-struck teenager gaping at the homecoming king.

Adria patted her knee again. "Of course it is."

Tori didn't bother to deny it. There'd be no point. She certainly didn't seem to be fooling the woman. Obviously, Tori wore her heart on her sleeve and her emotions on her face. "Is it that obvious?" she asked on a defeated sigh.

Adria's small laugh wasn't unkind. "Yes. For

what it's worth, he keeps looking over here at you, too."

Probably just curious as to what she was talking to his sister about.

Tori ducked her head. How had she even gotten here? When had she fallen so hard? She could blame Eloise. All her talk about taking chances, how she would give Tori the wedding dress she'd be married in when it was her turn. Her sister had put dreamy ideas into her head, and look where she found herself. Hopelessly in love with a man she had no chance of a future with.

Adria gave her a conspiratorial wink. "Don't worry. I'll keep your secret just as well as you're keeping mine."

CHAPTER NINE

How did a man look so sexy and tempting carrying a squirming, soaking wet toddler?

Tori's eyes were starting to ache from forcing them to look in any direction but where he stood. Clay hoisted his niece over his shoulder and climbed the steps out of the pool. Water gleamed like spun gold over his tanned skin. His hair was wet and fell in haphazard curls over his forehead.

She had to suck in a gasp of longing. Adria must have heard, as she could have sworn the woman chuckled under her breath.

"Hey," he said by way of greeting as he reached their side.

"Hey, yourself." Tori nearly groaned out loud. Way to come back with a witty response.

He flashed her that smile with a head tilt that always brought a flush to her skin. He slid on a pair of stylish sunglasses that made it difficult to gauge his expression. By contrast, he could no doubt read all the desire and longing swimming in her own eyes.

"Want to hand me that?" he said, pointing to something behind her.

For a second, Tori had no clue what he may be referring to. She glanced around. Did he want the lemonade pitcher?

Why was she suddenly such a frazzled mess around him?

The answer was obvious, of course. She'd spent the night in his arms, enjoying fully every pleasurable moment he gave her. Now, she couldn't deny just how much she wanted him to touch her that way again.

"The towel," he clarified.

"Oh! Of course. Here."

He had to be silently laughing at her. She didn't dare look in Adria's direction as she tossed him the towel. He expertly wrapped it around Lilly and began drying her off.

For a single bachelor who led a pretty busy life, he certainly seemed to know how to handle a toddler. Especially impressive considering he'd only been an uncle for under three years. And look how well he'd taken care of his sisters at such a high cost to himself. He'd essentially put himself in the line of fire to keep them safe.

She had no doubt in her mind, despite his nightmare of a childhood, that Clay would make an excellent father someday. Caring and attentive, he was beyond patient with Lilly.

Stop right this minute.

Thoughts like that were not going to lead anywhere good. The last thing she needed was to picture Clay as a father. To imagine dark-haired, olive-skinned little tykes who had their father's deep chocolate-brown eyes and perhaps her angular, dimpled chin.

Heavens. What in the world was wrong with her?

He'd offered her nothing more than a temporary physical fling. And here she was, fantasizing about having his babies. It was so uncharacteristic of her, it was totally disconcerting.

She looked up to find Adria studying her. "Are you all right, Tori? You've suddenly gone rather red."

"It is rather hot," Tori hedged. She wasn't overheated. She was blushing at the direction her wayward mind had just taken her.

Tori gave her head a shake to clear the useless images.

She could use a good dip in the pool herself. Though it probably wouldn't do much to cool her off.

* * *

She looked so cute when she was frazzled. Then again, Clay couldn't recall a time when she didn't look adorable. Even those times he'd seen her covered in sugar and flour, her apron stained.

Now, Tori seemed to be doing everything she could to avoid making eye contact with him. Was she thinking of all the ways he'd touched her last night? And all the ways she'd touched him? He, for one, hadn't been able to stop thinking about it.

She leaned over to address Lilly. "How was your swim?"

"Good," Lilly answered then stuck two fingers into her mouth.

"It wasn't so much a swim as an upper arm workout for her uncle," Adria quipped, handing her daughter a sippy cup full of lemonade.

Clay used the towel to try to dry himself off. It was hardly worth the effort, already soaked from Lilly's splashing. What he wanted to do, what he wouldn't have hesitated to do if his sister and niece weren't present, was to wrap the towel around Tori and use it to pull her to him. Then he would take her lips with his own…

But they weren't alone. Not to mention they were at the resort pool with several guests and workers meandering around.

"Cu'cake waydee!" Lilly announced, pointing to Tori with a toothless smile.

Tori's smile in return was brilliant and genuine. "That's right. I'm the cupcake lady."

Lilly nestled closer to her and tried to climb onto her lap. Tori didn't hesitate. Gently lifting the girl, she set her on her lap with an amused laugh. "I guess that makes me okay in your book, huh?"

Clay could hardly wait to take her into his own lap. She was pretty okay in his book, too. He sat next to them on the lounger. The smell of her coconut lotion and rose shampoo tickled his nostrils. He'd absorbed those scents so deeply last night.

Adria handed him a sweaty glass of lemonade and he took it gratefully, briefly considering dumping it over his head rather than drinking it. Lilly would sure get a kick out of it if he did that. But then he'd have to explain that he felt hot and bothered by the woman next to him—the cupcake lady herself. If he was smart, he would just get up and leave. He'd done his good deed by his sister. He could reward himself with a cold shower in his room.

Suddenly music filled the air and an exuberant resort employee jogged into the pool area. Wearing a bright yellow wig and enormous joke shop sunglasses, she asked the pool-goers, "Are you ready for a pool party?"

Lilly started clapping and scrambled to move off the lounger. "Yay!"

"It's kiddie dance time," Adria explained with a weary smile, slowly beginning to stand. Her voice said the last thing she was up for at the moment was play dancing by the pool to bouncy reggae versions of nursery songs.

Tori must have picked up on her lack of enthusiasm. "I can dance with her."

Adria's shoulders sagged with relief. "Oh, Tori. That would be fantastic. If you're sure you're up for it."

What was up with her? he wondered. She was usually much more energetic. Clay hardly recognized the sluggish, exhausted woman with the dark circles under her eyes.

"I would love to dance to 'Itsy Bitsy Spider' played on the steel drums with this young lady." Rising from the lounger, she took Lilly by the hand.

"Unca' Cway, too!" Lilly shouted and reached for his hand. Looked like he was on the hook.

With a resigned sigh, he let Lilly lead him and Tori to the other side of the pool where several other tots were already stomping tiny feet and pumping small arms.

Clay did his best version of the chicken dance then the electric slide. Judging by the way Tori laughed at him, his moves weren't impressing her. On the other hand, he couldn't stop watching her. Tori had a natural way to move to the music, her feet perfectly in sync with the beat. The pleasure on her face was captivating. Lilly's version of dancing was to run around the two of them while stomping her feet as hard as she could.

If someone had told him a week ago that he'd be dancing to kiddie reggae with the pretty baker from the North End by a pool while his niece ran around their legs, he might have wondered about their mental state.

The music outlasted Lilly's energy. Clay sensed the very moment she began to peter out and picked her up before she fell over from exhaustion.

Adria was already packing up when they walked back over to their chairs. "Thank you. Both of you." She threw the beach bag over her shoulder and took Lilly from Clay's arms. The child snuggled against her mother and fell asleep instantly on her shoulder.

"That had to be the most restful afternoon I've spent since we arrived here," Adria added in a soft whisper before walking away.

Again, it was fairly uncharacteristic of Adria

to make such a statement. She was one of those people who was constantly on the move, with energy to spare. He would have to ask her exactly what was going on. There had to be something besides the recent strain on their relationship and all that was happening with Enrique's career prospects. Not to mention the whole chaos of the wedding.

But right now, his focus was solely honed on Tori. He was finally about to get her alone. He had no doubt she was thinking the same thing, and got all the confirmation he needed when she bit her lower lip, as she had a habit of doing.

No words needed to be said between them. Gently taking her hand, he silently led her from the pool area and along the path that led to his room.

When they finally reached the door and shut it behind them, it was a scramble to relieve her of her clothes.

"I thought I'd never get you to myself," he rasped against her cheek before trailing kisses along her neck and shoulder. Tori's response was a low-level groan that broke the last thread of his control.

Later, with her curled up against his side and the light breeze from an open window carrying the sound of the ocean through the air, he whispered softly in her ear. "Tori?"

"Yes?"

"I really love the way you dance."

"Even to kiddie reggae?"

"Absolutely."

She giggled softly, nestled closer against him. "Oh. Um…well, thanks, I guess."

"Any man who doesn't is a fool."

He hadn't meant to say that out loud.

She didn't think she was ever going to get enough of this man.

They'd opted for room service in Clay's room rather than venturing out again. That was fine with her. She could handle a few more stolen moments with Clay. Considering this was all so temporary, that it would end in just a couple short days, she would take what she could get.

The thought settled like a brick of disappointment in her stomach, so she pushed it away. For now, she would live in the moment. Enjoy the company of the man she'd somehow fallen head over heels in love with.

There was no denying that any longer.

Clay handed her a glass of wine and removed the covers from the plates on the serving trolley that had arrived only moments before. A hot curl of steam rose into the air along with the smell of lemon, exotic spices and roasted chicken.

"Hmm. A girl could get used to this," she said, unfolding a napkin onto her lap. Except that was a lie. She really couldn't get used to it, tempting as this was. At some point, she would be going back to reality. A reality that only held Clayton Ramos in her memories— until he called with an order.

Stop it already.

Why couldn't she just let go of all these pestering thoughts and enjoy herself? Live for the moment, like Eloise so often suggested?

"You spoil me," she added playfully. Her reward was a passionate kiss that almost had her suggesting they forget about the food.

"Anything for the cupcake lady," Clay teased.

The reminder of the afternoon with Lilly brought a smile to her lips. "Your niece is absolutely adorable. But you know that, don't you?"

She wondered how he would feel when he finally learned that his uncle duties were about to double. Chances were strong that Tori wouldn't be in his life when the news was announced. Another pang of hurt tugged at her heart.

She couldn't seem to stop herself with the

defeatist and depressing thoughts. Yet she couldn't help but consider how all this would affect the days to come. How exactly did one embrace carpe diem when they'd been living their whole lives with the complete opposite mindset until now?

"She is pretty cute," Clay said around a mouthful of food. "And she really seems to have taken a liking to you."

"That's because she associates me with small cakes and sugary frosting."

He shrugged. "Maybe. Or maybe she's a real good judge of character for a three-year-old."

It was silly to feel so touched by such an innocuous compliment. But Tori felt her chest swell just the same. "You're really good with her," she returned with a compliment of her own. It was the absolute truth. "Lilly's lucky to have an uncle like you."

"The kid could have done worse, I suppose. It's not like I have anyone else to spoil." He paused to sip his wine. "Or like I ever will."

She knew she shouldn't ask, knew without a doubt that she wasn't going to like the answer he would return. But she couldn't seem to help herself. "Does that mean you wouldn't ever want that for yourself? To be a parent." She swallowed, then added, "Or to be someone's husband?"

He visibly shuddered at the thought and Tori wanted to kick herself. She should have never even ventured down this path.

"Marriage and kids aren't for people like me," Clay told her.

She tried to sound unaffected by his answer, while inside she shook with hurt and disappointment, recalling how the conversation seemed to echo the very thoughts she'd had by the pool earlier.

Clay continued. "Marriage is for guys like Tom. Or Enrique. Guys who enjoyed the safety of stable homes. Guys who didn't have to grow up too soon." He poured more wine for both of them before adding, "A man like me is much better off sticking with uncle-hood."

Well, she'd asked the question and now she had her answer. Not that she spent her days pining for a future with the proverbial white picket fence, but she knew that at some point in her life she did want a family. A family like the one she'd grown up in, with loud meals and messy fights and tons of love and laughter.

She wanted what Adria had. She wanted a wedding like Gemma was about to enjoy, secure in the knowledge that she'd found a man who cherished her. A man who wanted to spend the rest of his life with her. She wanted what her sister had so recently found.

She also wanted Clay.

And all those things were mutually exclusive.

What did it matter? It wasn't as if she would be given any kind of choice in the matter. Clay hadn't so much as made one mention of how things between them might play out once they returned to the States.

In fact, he'd made it clear before they'd spent their first night together that what they had would be no more than physical. Not as far as he was concerned, anyway.

Suddenly, Tori found she no longer had an appetite. The roast chicken that had her stomach grumbling and her mouth watering just moments ago suddenly tasted like cardboard in her mouth. Even the sip of wine she'd just taken lodged like a slip of wet paper in her throat.

If Clay noticed the change in her demeanor, he didn't make any comment.

Or maybe he didn't care to notice.

It appeared neither one of them could sleep.

Clay watched silently as Tori left the bed and made her way to the balcony. Whatever was on her mind, she'd been tossing and turning since they'd retired at midnight. He debated leaving her to herself. She was probably just looking to clear her head.

But several minutes passed and his curiosity won out. At least, that's what he told himself.

The truth? He was trying to conveniently ignore the nagging feeling that his bed felt lonely without her in it.

And that wouldn't do at all. He just didn't know what he was going to do about it when the time came.

She started a little when he opened the door and joined her where she leaned against the balcony railing, staring out into the starlit sky.

"Do I snore or is something else keeping you from sleeping?" he asked, taking her in his arms from behind, her back against his chest. He couldn't seem to stop wanting to touch her.

She indulged him with a light chuckle, almost too low to hear over the gentle lapping of the waves in the distance. "Like a freight train."

If only he could somehow capture this moment, stop it in time. Everything was perfect as is.

Too bad the world had to keep turning.

"If I promise to be quiet, will you come back to bed?" he breathed against her ear.

"I lied. You do not snore. I was just admiring the night sky. So many stars shining like faraway diamonds."

"It's a beautiful sight." A poet, he wasn't. Nor was he the type to stand around admiring the stars above. But Tori was good at making him take note of things he normally wouldn't have.

"I love New England," she told him. "But the view here in the tropics is something out of a dream."

She continued. "My family owns a very small place on the beach. We go for a couple weeks every summer. Been doing so since I can remember, with my parents commuting to the restaurant on weekends."

Clay chuckled. "Weekends by the beach without parental supervision? I'm guessing you and your brothers got into all sorts of trouble."

She shook her head. "They co-own the house with my aunt and uncle. So adults were always present. Along with my four cousins. It gets crowded, but there's no shortage of fun. Even now that we're all adults ourselves."

"Sounds like a great way to spend summers." Not for the first time since meeting her, Clay pondered what it must have been like to belong to such a large family. To feel part of a tight-knit group that spent weekends on the beach together in a tiny house.

"Josh often came with us, too. Along with—"

She'd stopped midsentence, but he could guess who she'd been about to refer to.

"Ah, the ex." Without thought, he wrapped his arms snugly around her middle. The scent of her shampoo ticked his nose and he nuzzled her hair indulgently.

"Yes. Drew often came along with us."

Dislike and resentment for a man he'd never met and wouldn't recognize on the street swamped his gut. The thought of Tori with someone else left a bitter taste in his mouth. How utterly Neanderthal, but he couldn't help what he couldn't help.

"The funny thing is, I wasn't even the one who invited him along."

He pulled back in surprise. "You weren't?"

"No. I was actually looking for a few days apart. Summers seemed to be the only time that could happen."

"Then how was he there?"

She sighed, rubbed her forehead. He could feel her muscles stiffen under his touch. "My brother Ty invited him one year. And it seemed to become a tradition after that. They were all friends."

"Sounds like you two dated for a long time." A tendril of unease uncurled within him. He had to acknowledge it as jealousy.

"Since high school."

"High school sweethearts." The bitterness on his tongue grew stronger.

"Everyone thought I was crazy to break up with someone like him." Her voice sounded low and raspy. "But I knew I couldn't be who I was meant to be if I stayed."

"Meaning?"

She sighed. "Drew has a very strong personality. He didn't want me to go away to school. He didn't want me to spend my free time with anyone but him. I only had one good friend through school. Shawna was the only one who didn't care what Drew thought and stuck around." An affectionate tone slipped into her voice. "It all came to a head when I decided to open the bakery."

"How so?" Clay asked, though he figured he could guess. Men like her ex didn't often want to share their time. Especially when it came to pursuing their own dreams.

"He said I was foolish to even attempt it. That I was too young, too inexperienced. That I was doomed to fail. He told me he was doing me a favor in trying to discourage me."

"Yet you proved him wrong." Man, had she ever. A surge of pride shot through him, though it made no sense. He had no claim to her or to her professional success.

She turned her head to look at him over her shoulder. Even in the dark, he could see the brilliance of her smile. "I sure did, didn't I?"

Her earlier wording troubled him. "What did you mean when you said 'things came to a head'?"

Her chin lifted, set with strength and sheer grit as she settled back against his chest. "He never physically hurt me."

His vision grew dark at even the thought.

Tori gave her head a shake. "It's just... There was the time he pulled me away from the dance floor a little too abruptly at a party, his grip on my wrist a little tighter than usual. It happened after an argument we'd had. He'd said I was foolish for taking on so much debt with a business loan."

Clay's arms instinctively enveloped her as she continued. "I knew right then I had to walk away. Without looking back."

His response was to turn her in his arms and take her lips with his own, indulging in a kiss that had them both moaning out loud.

Clay lost sight of how long they stood out there, simply admiring the night. Even as the first early rays of dawn broke the sky, he was hesitant to let her go. Finally, after about Tori's third contagious yawn, he took her by the hand and led her back inside.

She fell asleep in his arms moments later. But sleep eluded him as he mulled over everything she'd told him about her former lover. The thought of any man treating her in any derogatory way made him want to punch a wall. He knew who he'd be thinking of as he threw that punch, too.

He'd never considered himself to be a violent man. Saints knew he'd been tempted often enough, especially as the years passed and he'd grown taller and gained some muscle. He'd managed to somehow always hold the anger at bay. But right at this moment, he couldn't say for certain what he might do if he ever crossed paths with Tori's former boyfriend.

The guy bore more than a striking resemblance to the man who had crashed into Clay's life without warning. Personality wise, at least. In Tori's description of her ex, Clay had detected several common characteristics—controlling, belittling, and demanding. A man who always had to have his own way.

A man just like the monster he'd had to grow up with.

Tori woke hours later in Clay's arms and allowed herself to simply feel his strength around her. The scents of sandalwood and mint that she was now so fond of flooded her nose and she breathed them in, deeply indulging in the familiarity.

She felt safe in his embrace, coveted.

She'd fallen asleep rather shaken. Divulging all she had about Drew had taken a lot out of her. As a result, her slumber had been restless and flitting.

"Bad dreams?" Clay asked softly in her ear. "You were tossing and turning a lot."

Now that he mentioned it, she realized a nightmare had indeed been what had roused her. "Yes. I'm sorry if I woke you."

He gently took her by the shoulder and rolled her over to face him. "Tell me what's up."

Tori nestled closer against his chest, allowing herself the full comfort of his warm embrace. "Just a lot of bad memories. Triggered by our conversation earlier."

"It might help to talk some more, then. I have wide shoulders, Tori. And when it comes to you, I'm all ears."

She took a deep breath. Maybe it *would* help to get it all off her chest finally. Her emotions were like a sea of violent waves when it came to her past relationship. And here was Clay, offering her a safe harbor. At least for a little while.

"He was my first boyfriend..." she began.

"We were both juniors. I couldn't believe a boy would notice me. Let alone a boy like him."

"Big man on campus?"

"Complete with all the letters and captain-ships. While I was a bit of a loner."

He sniffed her hair. "I find that hard to believe, given what I know of you now."

"It's true. I never really felt comfortable in my own skin. Always felt like there was a piece of me missing." A chill ran down her spine. "I have to wonder now if it was some sixth sense telling me there was a sibling out there who could help me be complete."

"Oh, Tori."

"Everyone kept telling me how lucky I was. Especially all the girls who would have done anything to date him. And I believed them. I was too young to realize the effect the relation-ship was having on me."

"How so?"

Tori squeezed her eyes shut. "I started to change. Began dressing differently. I grew my hair long when I'd always preferred it short."

"I love your short, spiky hair."

"He said it didn't suit me."

Clay's entire body stiffened next to hers. "He was wrong."

"I know that now. But at the time I just

wanted to please this boy who had miraculously chosen me. So I did what he told me."

"What else?" Clay prodded.

"He asked me to sign up for the same classes so that we could study together." She humphed a bitter laugh. "Free tutoring for him would be a more accurate way to describe it."

The memories came flashing back on a wave of regret. She'd lost so many days of her youth trying to accommodate someone else's wishes. But it could have been so much worse. She could consider herself lucky.

"By the time we graduated high school and attended college, he was fully ingrained in my life. My brothers and parents loved him. They only saw the friendly, charming side that he was so good at projecting. He could be quite clever." Her family still didn't understand why she'd turned her back on what they'd seen as an ideal life partner.

"What happened then? After you started university?"

"I was studying hospitality and restaurant management, but my heart wasn't in it. I love working for my parents at the trattoria. But it wasn't a lifelong goal. I started baking for fun. Then I took a baking class as an elective."

"And the rest is history."

She ran a finger up his chest and over his

shoulder, just to be able to touch him, to feel his warmth on her fingertips. "It was the beginning of the end for me and Drew. He took it as a personal betrayal when I quit school to open up a bakery. I took out loans, both personal and business. He said no wife of his was going to go into debt and waste her talents. I knew right then without any doubt that I absolutely did not want to be his wife. And I told him as much."

Clay let out a low whistle.

"That's when his behavior started to grow more and more aggressive and hostile."

"So you got out."

"I had to. I would have lost myself if I'd stayed with him."

He pecked a kiss to the top of her head. "But you didn't stay with him. And look at all you've accomplished since. You're a household name in your field. You've put your heart and soul into a lifestyle that you love. You're the very definition of success, Tori. Despite how hard he tried to stop you."

Tori ducked her head under his chin and kissed the side of his neck. His pulse throbbed against her lips. When he spoke that way and held her tight in his arms, she could almost believe him.

CHAPTER TEN

THE MERINGUE WAS the key to the whole thing.

If the meringue was imperfect in any way, too soggy or too stiff, the whole thing would fall apart. Quite literally.

Tori bit her lip and focused on the job at hand. She had to get the consistency just right. The top layer of Gemma's cake was supposed to be a confectionary replica of the Leaning Tower of Pisa, the historic landmark in Italy where Gemma and Tom had taken their first vacation together.

She'd been having trouble concentrating all day. Clay was the one to blame for that. Tori couldn't seem to get him out of her mind. And she would tell him so as soon as she laid eyes on him again.

Focus.

The cake wasn't going to make itself.

It took her three more tries to get the consistency just right. Then she was on her way.

By this time tomorrow, a masterpiece—if she did say so herself—of a wedding cake with five tiers topped by a molded sponge cake replica of an Italian landmark would be the centerpiece of a festive marital ceremony.

A ceremony she wasn't invited to.

Tori pushed the thought aside. She was here to do a job, not attend a party. Regardless of what was happening between her and the bride's brother.

Not that she could define exactly what was happening between them. She'd never before shared with anyone the specifics about how Drew had treated her toward the end of their relationship. Not even Eloise. Clay had listened to her last night without any judgement. She hadn't realized exactly how much she'd needed that from someone. On a deep-seated level, she knew she had no blame for the way Drew had behaved toward her. But a tiny yet not silent part of her wondered how she'd ever let things get that far.

Why had she stayed? Even past the point where she'd known the relationship was hopeless, known that she hadn't loved Drew. And perhaps never had.

She'd been half afraid Clay would ask her

that last night—if she'd loved Drew. Luckily he hadn't. She wasn't sure how she might have answered.

Hours later, Tori had all the pieces baked and cooling on various racks. All that was left was to assemble the cake, which could be done tomorrow morning.

And her job here would be done. Meaning her time here on the island was coming to an end, as well. She bit back a sob then silently reprimanded herself for being so foolish. She'd known what she was getting into. Clay had been nothing but straight with her from the beginning.

And she'd gone and fallen in love with him anyway.

As if her thoughts had prompted it, her cell phone pinged with a text message. Clay's profile appeared on the screen.

Where are you? Kitchen?

She answered then waited for the dancing dots to transform into words.

Is this a good time to stop by?

Yes. Timing couldn't be better, in fact.

Good. Have to ask you something. I need a favor.

???

Will explain when I get there.

Tori was about to put the phone back in her apron pocket when it pinged with yet another message. This one flooded her heart with warmth. And also with a heavy dose of sadness at what might have been if things had been different.

Miss you.

Yeah. Adria had been absolutely right yesterday by the pool. Tori did indeed have it bad.

The few minutes it took for Clay to arrive felt like eons. What kind of favor was he looking for exactly? Tori's curiosity heightened with each passing second until he finally showed up. He'd recently showered, she could tell. His hair was wet and combed back, his skin still damp and fresh.

Even casually dressed in plain khaki shorts and a fitted V-necked T-shirt, the man looked like he could walk down a runway in Milan.

While here she was covered in flour and sugar and wearing a frumpy apron.

"What is that heavenly smell?" he asked, taking her by the hand and pulling her to him for a deep and lingering kiss that had her momentarily breathless.

She cleared her throat when she could find her voice again. "Well, it could be the meringue. Or the sponge candy used to make the tower. Or you might be referring to the buttercream frosting."

He flashed her a devilish grin. "Or it could be you."

The man certainly was a charmer. He grabbed her sketch pad from where it lay open on the counter and studied her drawing of the wedding cake.

"So this is the final plan, huh?"

She nodded.

"How in the world are you going to get it to stand upright, especially when the top is literally supposed to lean over?"

She pointed to the spots she'd drawn at strategic points on the pastry.

"Huh. This is a lot like architecture." He tapped her nose. "I make exactly those kinds of decisions when designing buildings. We have more in common than we even knew."

He flashed her that dizzyingly handsome smile of his. "We'd make a great team."

He had to stop saying those things to her. Every such comment made her long for the future they might have had. For what could be between them if only he were open enough to consider it.

But Clay had decided long ago that he was going to close himself off. And Tori didn't have it in her to twist herself into some kind of pretzel to accommodate a man who was supposed to love her and accept her as she was.

Been there, done that.

She pulled the sketch pad back and closed it, perhaps a little too abruptly. "Yes. Well, let's hope it works. It's never a certainty."

He blinked at her in question. "I have no doubt that it will. I have faith in your abilities."

Yet more compliments. "So, what's this favor you need?"

"I've been asked to babysit again. Lilly needs someone to accompany her to an activity."

"Is Adria not feeling well?" She'd been meaning to check on his sister but time had gotten away from her. Poor thing really seemed to be having a tough first trimester.

"Yeah. I'm wondering if she picked up a bug

or something on the way here. Everyone else seems to be doing fine, though."

Tori made sure to remain silent.

"And Enrique is stuck on another phone call with his agent and his club. Sounds like negotiations aren't going very well."

"That's too bad." One more thing for Adria to have to deal with. She'd be sure to give her a call as soon as she had a moment.

"I'd rather have some help with this one. Not sure I trust myself to take it on alone. And I guess they've already paid for it and have talked it up to Lilly. They don't want to let her down."

Whatever he was referring to sounded like a bit more than an afternoon of face painting or craft of some sort. "What kind of activity are we talking about here?"

He leaned in closer to her over the counter. "Tell me, how do you feel about dolphins?"

She looked pretty darn sexy in a wet suit.

Clay had been nervous back there for a while when it looked like Tori might not want to join them. She'd certainly taken long enough to answer. In the end, much to his relief, she'd finally agreed. Clay hadn't exactly been looking forward to wrangling his toddler niece by himself in a small cay with oversize fish circling them, trained or not.

Admit it, a little voice goaded in his head. *You just wanted her here.*

"I've never been swimming with dolphins before," Tori said next to him in the aquatics hut slash gift store. Souvenirs like stuffed dolphins and sea turtle keychains surrounded them.

The animal trainer was given instructions about exactly what to expect and all the safety precautions to be adhered to once everyone was in the water.

Lilly made it hard to pay attention. She'd made it a game to demand going from Tori's lap back to his repeatedly. Not to mention how distracted he was by Tori's enticing curves in that suit. Finally, Tori gently started to stroke the little girl's hair, which somehow soothed her enough to settle down.

About twenty minutes later, they followed the pleasant young aquatics trainer, Liv, to a small cay with crystal-blue water.

Liv blew her whistle and they waited for the show to start. And waited. Nothing seemed to be happening.

"Sometimes they take their time," Liv told them rather apologetically.

Remarkably, Lilly noticed it before either

of them. She pointed a wet finger toward the water. "Fish."

Sure enough, the water rippled several feet in front of them as a silvery gray fin glided along the surface. Suddenly, a dolphin's head popped up so close Clay could reach out and touch it. Lilly clapped with glee from where Tori still held her on one hip. For her part, Tori looked pretty entranced herself.

He'd be hard pressed to decide which of them seemed more excited, in fact. Both Tori and his niece had matching expressions of wonder. Not everyone could be patient when it came to unruly, energetic toddlers.

Tori was beyond good with Lilly.

Yeah, he was really glad she hadn't turned him down.

Tori held Lilly cozily in her arms as they watched the dolphins play in the water. When the trainer blew her whistle and twirled her hand, they spun around upright in the water then landed with a splash. Lilly erupted in excited laughter every time they were doused with spray.

Now, Liv was pumping her hand up and down in the air. The dolphins started bobbing in and out of the water in response.

"This is quite a show," Clay said, a smile

of utter joy on his face. He looked boyish and carefree. Tori had to wonder how many days during his childhood he could recall as totally untroubled.

How many days had he been able to spend riding a bike or tossing a ball or just lazily wasting the hours? Instead of mourning the loss of his father and dodging a bully.

"Ah, one of the dolphins has decided to leave us," Liv told them, her accent charming. "We never force the dolphins to do anything. They come if they please and stay for as long as they please."

Liv turned to Lilly after reaching for something in one of the pockets on her utility belt. "This one must be hungry." She pointed to the remaining dolphin. "I'm guessing that's why she didn't follow her friend when he swam off. Would you like to help your mommy feed her?"

"Oh, I'm not—"

But the young woman wasn't listening. Handing Tori and Lilly a small bait fish of some kind, she instructed, "Hold your hand out like this."

To Tori's delight, the remaining dolphin swam up slowly and gently took the offering from her hand.

"She likes you," Liv said and then turned to face Clay. "Would you like to feed her, too?"

Clay shook his head with a wide smile. "No, that's okay. I think my two ladies here have it under control."

Tori didn't even allow herself to lament on that statement. His ladies. She'd rather focus on the delightful scene in front of her.

"She wants to be petted," Liv explained. "It's why she's staying so close to you."

Tori gingerly reached out her hand, still balancing Lilly on her hip. Ever so softly, she touched the surface of the animal's back. Its skin felt like wet velvet, and it made no move to swim away.

"She really likes you!" Liv exclaimed, handing her another fish. This time, Tori took Lilly's hand in hers when she extended the treat to the dolphin. The child squealed in delight when the fish took the food and flung its head back.

Lilly suddenly threw her arms around Tori's neck and gave a squeeze. "Wiwwy wikes Towi, too."

It took a moment to figure out what the little girl had just said. When she did, Tori's heart felt like it had swollen to twice its size. *Lilly likes Tori, too.*

She nuzzled the top of the toddler's head

with her cheek, and gave her a small kiss on the top of her wet curls. "I like you, too, sweetheart. Very much."

Heaven help her, she'd somehow grown attached to his niece as well as to the man himself.

CHAPTER ELEVEN

"Who's up for some ice cream?" Clay asked from above her head where Tori sat drying Lilly off and getting her dressed.

She'd been tending to the little girl while Clay had gone off to buy half the gift shop, it seemed. He could barely hold all the packages in both arms. It was clear he liked to spoil the little girl, but all the purchases seemed a bit excessive.

"Who is that all for? Seems too much for one little girl."

He blinked at her. "I founded and help run Our New Start, remember? I figured the kids might get a kick out of some of these. I plan to ship them out tomorrow."

Tori didn't know whether to laugh or cry. At every turn, she seemed to experience something new or to find out something more that pulled her further toward the wonder that was Clay Ramos. Not only had he founded the charity, he was hands on enough to purchase toys for it. Just one more layer of frosting on the cake.

How in the world would she ever go about forgetting him?

"So how about it?" he addressed Lilly. "You up for some chocolate-chip ice cream with fudge on top?"

"Yay!"

Fifteen minutes later, they sat at a picnic table by the resort's ice cream parlor. A ground-level fountain intermittently shot out streams of neon-colored water a few feet away. Lilly was transfixed as she watched it, jumping into Tori's arms every time the water erupted into the air.

She was also covered from head to toe in sticky, gooey ice cream. Adria hadn't seemed the type to fret over such things. And her uncle certainly didn't seem concerned about the messy state of his niece.

Tori looked up to find two familiar faces approaching them. "Aun' Geya!" Lilly yelled, squirming to free herself.

"That's right. It's Aunt Gemma." Gemma walked over to the toddler and picked her up to give her a tight hug. "I'd kiss you but I don't like chocolate ice cream," she told her.

Tom and Clay did some kind of masculine handshake by way of greeting.

"How about I take this little rug rat off your hands and get her cleaned up?"

Tori looked up to find Gemma actually addressing her with the question. "Uh, I guess it's up to Clay."

"What do say, big bro? Had enough of this little bossy tyrant yet?"

"I suppose so."

"You need a bath." Before walking away, Gemma suddenly turned. "I can't wait to see that cake, Tori."

"Come by tomorrow before you start getting ready, if you'd like. I'll have it all assembled and chilling in the refrigerator."

Gemma shook her head. "Nope, I'd rather see it when it's unveiled at the wedding. You can witness firsthand my awed impression of your creation."

That sounded as though Gemma expected her to be there. Had she missed something? She certainly didn't recall receiving any kind of invite.

This was certainly awkward. "Oh. I, uh, didn't realize I was supposed to be in attendance."

Gemma's eyes narrowed and her jaw actually dropped. "Of course you're going to be there, Tori. At the wedding as well as the rehearsal dinner, in fact. As a guest of the bride herself. I insist. The only reason I didn't say anything was that I figured my clueless sibling here would have taken care of inviting you himself already." She rolled her eyes in Clay's direction then turned to Tori once more. "Wait till you see my dress."

Okay. So she wasn't expected to be at the wedding as some kind of employee then. Tori snuck a glance at Clay.

He didn't look up from his sundae.

If the past few moments had been awkward, things didn't get any better after Gemma and Tom walked away, Lilly in tow.

Tori continued spooning her cup of Rocky Road but wasn't really tasting it.

Clay didn't seem to be in any kind of hurry to talk, either.

Did he even want her at the wedding? The silence between them right now seemed to indicate the answer to that was a resounding no.

"Hope Adria's feeling better," she began, just to get some conversation flowing.

"I'm sure she's fine. I'll check on her before I head back to the room."

"Please give her my best."

"Sure."

"She certainly seems to have a lot on her

mind on top of having to keep up with an active toddler. Between her husband's contract dealings, the excitement of her sister's wedding, and renewed contact with her estranged mother…"

Tori wasn't even sure why she brought up that last topic. Just that she really didn't think the situation involving their mother was helping matters as far as Adria's stress level was concerned. If there was any chance that his sister might feel better physically if the issue were somehow addressed, wasn't it worth pursuing?

The shadow that fell over Clay's face said he clearly felt differently.

His voice was cold and harsh when he spoke. "I don't see how that's a matter that you and I need to be discussing in any way."

Tori felt the chill of his words travel through her ears, down her spine, right clear to her toes.

In other words, it was none of her business. She'd clearly overstepped.

So she was good enough to share his bed, but apparently he drew the line at family events or even speaking of matters that concerned his family. A compelling urge to throw her now melted ice cream into his face nearly overwhelmed her good sense. Somehow she resisted, instead gripping the stem of the sundae glass so firmly her knuckles began to hurt. There was no use in sitting there, steaming with anger and feeling upset. And hurt.

"It's been a long day," she announced as she stood. "Thanks for taking me along on the dolphin adventure."

He gave a brisk nod of his head. "Sure thing. Hope you can get some rest."

He made no move to stop her from leaving.

What had just happened?

The mood of the afternoon had turned so quickly. Clay rose from the picnic table with a curse. The dolphin swim had been one of the most entertaining experiences of his life. Tori's face as she'd held Lilly in her arms to feed the dolphins would be an image ingrained in his mind forever. He hadn't been able to wait to get her alone to tell her just how tempting she'd looked in that wet suit.

But as soon as Tom and Gemma had showed up, an unsettling feeling had risen in his chest. Gemma had invited her to the wedding… Lilly had treated her like a beloved aunt she'd known her whole life… And it sounded like Adria had confided in her, at least on some level.

He had to take stock of it all. Having Tori

in their lives was a temporary state of affairs. Did his sisters not see that?

What exactly did they think was going to happen? That they would all get together once in a while and just include Tori in the plans? Invite her to family gatherings and barbecues?

Tori inquiring about Adria reconnecting with their estranged mother had completely caught him off guard. He had no intention of getting into all that with anyone. Not even Tori. He was still hoping Adria would drop the whole thing altogether. How could she not see how futile and damaging her quest was? Already it was leading to all sorts of conflicts and frazzled nerves.

Women. He'd probably never understand them.

One thing he did understand—in just a few short days, Tori had somehow become entrenched in all their lives. Not just his.

Somehow it had happened when he hadn't been paying attention.

But the way he'd snapped at her had been uncalled for. Gemma was right. He did want her at the wedding. He should have been the one to ask her.

He'd held back, procrastinated. For reasons that had nothing to do with Tori and everything to do with him.

It's not you, it's me.

The classic line of doomed relationships. Only in this case, it happened to be the truth.

By the time he got to his hotel room, Clay was feeling all the worse for snapping at Tori the way he had. Not like it was her fault she had the kind of personality that drew people to her and then made them want to stick around. Look at what had happened to him after spending such a short amount of time with her.

And therein was the problem, wasn't it?

The only person he was really annoyed with was himself. He'd fallen for her—which was completely not right. He had nothing to offer a woman like Tori. He had no intention of settling down or attaching himself to any one person. Not in the foreseeable future. Probably not ever.

Whereas everything Tori was, down to her very fiber, revolved around family and love, and the way she bonded so easily with those around her. She'd already been badly burned in the relationship department. He wouldn't be the bastard that did anything to further hurt her the way her previous boyfriend had.

He rubbed his forehead and cursed some more. *This.* This was exactly what he'd wanted to avoid. He'd experienced firsthand the dire ramifications that could arise when lovesick souls followed their desires without regard to the end results. Without regard to the effect their actions would have on those around them.

Entanglements and careless affairs only led to unneeded complications. Yet somehow she'd gotten under his skin when he hadn't been paying attention. He was a mess of emotions right now—anger, confusion and disappointment, mostly with himself for allowing things to get this far.

Tori deserved stability. She deserved commitment. And she deserved better than the likes of what he could offer her. She deserved someone who would be there for her, through thick and thin. Good times and bad. He just didn't have it in him to risk any more of the bad in his life.

Hell, he couldn't even be sure what city he'd be in from week to week. In fact, there was even now a project in Amsterdam that he'd been offered and had yet to formally reply to. A brand-new modern art museum.

Not that he had any intention of accepting. It would be a long-term contract, keeping him out of the States for the next several months. Maybe up to a year or more, depending on the progress.

His mind was running in circles and he had to find some kind of outlet. Pacing around the room like a caged animal only served to further frustrate him, spiking his blood pressure sky-high.

Getting out of here would be good start. The air might do him good. Throwing on a fresh pair of shorts and an athletic T-shirt, he grabbed his running shoes from the closet.

The day was already scorching hot when he got to the beach—probably too hot to run—but he wanted the punishment.

As grueling as it was, Clay pushed himself to run harder and faster, willing the strenuous exercise to somehow put his thoughts straight. The heat was bearable if he stopped to splash some ocean water on his face and neck. Finally, the endorphins started to kick in, a sense of calm and clarity gradually settling over his nerves, helping to finally start clearing his head.

He'd been running about half a mile when the realization hit him like an ocean wave. As the blood pounded through his system and his mind slowly began to clear, the answer became more and more obvious. Now that he really thought about it, he'd be a fool to turn down the Amsterdam offer. What if nothing like that ever came his way again?

The more his feet pounded the sand, the clearer everything became. His life in the

States would be waiting for him as soon as he was ready to return. Sure, he'd miss seeing his sisters, and not being able to see Lilly once or twice a week would leave a hole in his life. But it was temporary. Plus, he'd visit every chance he could.

As for anyone else? Well, there really wasn't anyone else, was there? Not really. He had no business thinking of Tori as a permanent fixture in his life. Better to make a clean break, mostly for her sake. And here was one more way to do exactly that.

Pulling out his cell phone, he called up the email with the offer he'd archived, then started typing out a reply he had no idea he'd even been considering just a few short hours ago.

Why not? He had nothing to lose.

He ignored the faint voice in his head that tried to argue that very point.

When Tori wanted to relax back home, or when she wanted to try to take her mind off of things after a stressful day, she soothed herself by testing new recipes. Or sometimes she'd bake one of the specialty pastries she knew by heart. The orderly sequence of steps and the precise measuring of the needed ingredients always served to settle her nerves and soothe her spirit.

She didn't have that option now. As much as she had access to the resort's kitchen, she couldn't very well just pop in there for her own personal use and start tossing ingredients together.

But she did have the option of a world-class spa located right on the premises. Additionally, she could think of one other person on the island who would benefit from a spa treatment, as well.

Picking up the phone, she dialed the number Adria had written on the napkin that first day.

Three hours later, she and Adria were walking out with fresh manicures, painted toenails and massage-loosened limbs.

"Oh, Tori. Thank you so much for suggesting that. I really needed it."

"Me, too. I'm glad you were able to come along."

"You really are too good to me, you know. You feed me when I'm nauseous, invite me to a luxurious spa day and you help my brother babysit my child. You're almost too good to be true."

At the mention of Clay, all of Tori's tenseness seemed to surge right back into her muscles. Not that she'd been able to take her mind off him for long. Even under the expert hand of the masseuse, she'd had to remind herself to breathe out the tension.

He hadn't contacted her since their ice cream date with Lilly earlier. What in the world had made her bring up Adria and his mother? She should have known better.

While his sister had done more than her share of talking as they'd had their nails and toes painted, a good portion of the conversation had been dedicated to how she'd found her mother through a popular website. Adria knew her brother was against any contact with their surviving parent, apparently even her husband had reservations.

Though the siblings were close, Tori had the impression there weren't too many heart-to-heart conversations among the Ramos clan.

"It was nice to have someone to talk to," Adria said, echoing Tori's thoughts and confirming her suspicions as they casually strolled along the concrete pathway to the residential cottages.

"I'm glad I could lend an ear."

She suddenly stopped and placed a hand on Tori's forearm. A sheen of tears appeared in her eyes. "Am I being selfish, Tori? Enrique's parents passed in a plane accident before we met. Is it so wrong for me to want my children to have at least one grandparent in their lives? Flawed as she may be."

Tori wished so badly to somehow comfort the poor woman. She had no idea what she would do in a similar situation.

"No. Not from where I'm standing. People do change. You deserve the chance to find out once and for all if your mother has." She covered Adria's hand with her own where it rested on her arm.

That's how Clay found them when he turned the corner around the spa building.

Tori commanded her jaw not to drop open at the sight of him. His golden skin glistened with sweat, chest heaving with the exertion of exercise, his T-shirt soaked. He appeared to have been running.

Maybe he'd felt the need to let off a little steam the same way she'd needed a release of tension.

"What are you two up to?" he asked, stopping in front of them. He bent with his hands on his knees to suck in some air. Even in his current state, he looked devastatingly handsome. Her heart was never going to recover having to get over a man like this.

"Just a bit of a girls' outing," his sister answered. "But I'm afraid I have to get going. Lilly's probably wondering where Mama is."

She patted her brother's cheek affectionately. "I'll leave you two to yourselves."

He pointed to her feet after his sister walked away, his breathing somewhat back to normal. "Nice color toes."

"Thanks. Adria and I just enjoyed a mani-pedi followed by a full body massage."

"You two seem to have really hit it off."

She shrugged. "Just figured she could use some pampering, that's all. I imagine being the mother of a toddler doesn't often leave much time for luxury." Not to mention being pregnant and exhausted, but her lips were sealed on that score. Keeping Adria's secret solely to herself was rather nerve-racking. What if she let it slip? She had enough on her hands with one Ramos cross with her at the moment.

She would apologize. There was no way around it. In her sympathy for Adria, she'd overstepped her bounds with Clay. If it would lessen some of this newfound tension between them, she'd be happy to issue a mea culpa.

"Do you want to sit together at the rehearsal dinner?" She'd blurted out the question before she could give herself time to think.

They only had a little time left here together on the island. She didn't want to spend it at odds with each other. Back in Boston, she knew Clay would be prepared to walk away from her and what they'd shared on the island.

"Yeah. Sure," he answered simply, wiping the sweat off his forehead with the back of his hand. As if she'd asked him if he wanted extra toppings on his pizza. "I should probably shower first."

"Yes. I'd appreciate it if you did."

That tease finally cracked a smile out of him, albeit a small one. "All right. Meet you back here around seven?"

So polite, so unaffected, so very casual. Clay was very deliberately putting distance between them. Any woman would have been able to sense it. "That sounds good," she answered then forced a fake smile.

Unlike last night, it was clear they wouldn't be enjoying a private room-service dinner in his room.

CHAPTER TWELVE

THE MASSIVE FIREPIT in the middle of the barbecue food court had been lit for the evening. The aroma of the burned wood, combined with the various scents of the myriad delicacies cooking around them, made for a pleasantly appetizing atmosphere.

In addition to her heaving plate of plantains and exotic fried greens, Tori was fully prepared to eat crow.

"Keeping it light this evening?" Clay asked as they took their seats among the rest of the rehearsal dinner guests at a wood table by the crackling fire.

The truth was, her stomach felt a little off, twisted with apprehension. She so missed the easy camaraderie they'd once had.

"Saving room for dessert. Looks like there's a chocolate tower being set up close to the beach. Along with a champagne fountain."

"We should check it out." He took in a forkful of pulled barbecue beef.

"I'd like that."

She waited until they'd both finished eating before breaching the proverbial elephant in the room. "Look, Clay, I want to tell you that I'm sorry. I didn't mean to overstep that way I did earlier. It's really none of my concern."

He sighed deeply and rubbed his forehead. "Thank you for saying that. And I apologize, too. I had no right to snap at you the way I did."

He looked so disappointed in himself that she felt compelled to defend him. "You didn't really snap."

"Yes, I did. And I have no excuse for it. Just been wound up a little tight lately. Which makes no sense considering I'm in paradise and in the company of a beautiful woman whose company I thoroughly enjoy."

Tori felt like the anvil had been removed from her shoulders. Her stomach muscles slowly unclenched. She hated being on the receiving end of his coldness. Even for the briefest period of time following their adventure with the dolphins in the cay.

"So, truce then?" She reached a hand toward him.

He took it but not to shake. Instead he gently pulled her close to give her a brief kiss on the lips. He tasted of slow-cooked beef, exotic spices and cold beer. As far as peace offerings went, Tori figured she could have done worse.

"How about we toast this new truce of ours with a glass of champagne and some chocolate?" Clay asked as he helped her out of her chair once the speeches had concluded.

"Best offer I've had all day."

Clay went to procure their flutes of bubbly while Tori prepared a tray of assorted fruit dipped in chocolate. Everything from luscious strawberries to thick bananas to plump cherries. She added some biscuits to round out the flavors.

They eschewed the crowds by the dessert table and took their bounty to an open cabana by the water. He pulled her down to lie beside him in the cushioned lounge chair.

A girl could get used to this.

She had no idea she was about to doze off until the flute fell from her hand to land with a thud on the sand under their lounger.

"Here, I'll get it." He reached over to grab it and his shirt rode up, revealing his lower back.

There was no mistaking the angry-looking scar above his left hipbone. Tori couldn't hide her gasp of horror.

He knew immediately that she'd seen it. He straightened and pulled her closer. "It's no big deal. Happened a long time ago."

"How did I not notice it when we… Can I ask how you got it?" She didn't want a repeat of earlier when she'd overstepped, but her heart was breaking for him. She desperately wanted to learn that maybe her horrible suspicions about how he'd gotten such a nasty wound were wrong.

He shrugged. "Courtesy of my bas—" He bit off the curse.

Tori's eyes burned with the hot sting of tears. She remained completely still in his arms, completely silent, giving him the choice as to how much he wanted to divulge. Rage and sorrow launched a war in her chest when he finally began to speak.

"I was about fourteen. He didn't like the way Adria baited a fishing line, started to get very angry. I went over and made sure to mess it up even worse. Somehow the pole found my skin." He scoffed. "None of us even wanted to go fishing. My mother made us, to try to get us to somehow bond with him. As if it was even possible."

"Oh, Clay." From everything he had shared so far, she'd known that it was bad. But what she was hearing now was the stuff of nightmares. "I'm so very sorry. What you must have endured."

"Like I said, it's all in the past. What matters is that it's over. He's long gone. And that I ensured he never, ever, laid a hand on either Gemma or Adria."

"Would he really have tried anything with either of them?" When she thought about the utter horror of what she was actually asking, she shuddered.

"Wasn't gonna take the risk."

So he'd done what he'd had to do.

"I didn't sleep well at night for many years. Always had one eye open and my ears alert," he continued.

"Were there no adults around who could help?"

"Not when she was always sticking up for him. Everyone just took their word for it whenever something went down."

His resistance to Adria's idea about reuniting with their mother made all the sense in the world now. He'd spent the better part of his childhood shielding his younger sisters from a monster and bearing the brunt of the abuse solely on his own.

All to protect them.

In many ways, he must have taken Adria's sudden interest in her mother to be nothing less than a betrayal. It didn't help that he had no clue that her newfound desire stemmed from the impending arrival of a new baby.

Her heart ached for both of them. And for Gemma, too.

The conversation had gotten too heavy and taken a turn he hadn't intended. He was usually more evasive whenever someone asked him about that scar. He usually did a better job at keeping it hidden. As well as any of the others.

Normally, he was better at finding ways to answer without really answering.

But he found he didn't want to lie to Tori. So he'd told her the whole ugly truth.

She was trying hard to hide it, but there was no doubt she was crying. He hated that she was hurting on his behalf. But confiding in her had felt surprisingly cathartic. He'd never told a soul about the fishing pole incident. And he and his sisters didn't talk about their shared past. All three considered the latter part of their childhood to be better off forgotten, each building their own sturdy walls to block out the most painful memories.

But Tori had somehow broken through his walls when he hadn't expected it. Gathering her closer in his embrace, he simply held her while they watched the sun set on the horizon over the crystal-blue water.

Now that he'd made his decision about the job offer, he felt a sense of peace and purpose. He'd make it public in due time. But for now, he just wanted to enjoy one more night in Tori's company, simply talking to her and just being with her. Probably for one final time.

The night grew darker and colder, the champagne and treats long consumed.

Finally, he gently lifted her and half carried her to his room, where they fell asleep in each other's arms. It was perhaps the most restful night he'd spent in as long as he could remember.

Too bad it would never happen again.

All eyes were on the gorgeous bride as she approached her eagerly awaiting groom. Except for Tori's. Tori's gaze was solely focused on the man walking the bride down the aisle.

Clay was dressed in casual khaki pants and a Hawaiian shirt as per the tropical theme of the ceremony. He looked so rakishly handsome that Tori felt her breath catch. She hadn't seen him since this morning, when she'd woken in his arms after falling asleep on his bed the night before.

Then she'd been a flurry of activity all day,

making sure the cake was still holding and refrigerated correctly. Afterward, she'd had to get dressed. Now that she was seeing him again, it occurred to her how empty the day had seemed without him. Not that a minute had gone by when she hadn't thought of him or wondered what he was up to.

Gemma was beaming as she approached her intended. Tom clutched his chest as she neared the pulpit on her brother's arm, his expression full of love and affection. The scene brought forth memories of her own sister's wedding where she'd been a bridesmaid. Josh and Eloise had looked equally as enamored with each other.

A pang of longing shot through her chest. Josh had surprised Eloise with a romantic proposal after sweeping her off her feet. Gemma and Tom had fallen in love after traveling through Italy together. Would she ever have that? Would a man ever commit himself to her that way? Her eyes automatically found him and she had to tear her gaze away before they filled with tears.

Clay gave his sister an affectionate pat on the arm as they stopped beside Tom. Then he stepped to the side, his hands clasped in front of him while the officiant began the process of transforming Gemma and Tom into husband and wife.

Though she felt ridiculous, Tori couldn't help the emotional tears that started rolling down her cheeks; she just couldn't hold them at bay any longer. Clay and his sisters had been through so much yet all three of them had become successful, loving, compassionate people. People she'd grown to care so much for in such a short period of time.

Somehow she was supposed to turn around and shut off all those feelings like some kind of light switch now that the week was coming to an end. Even the tender, amorous feelings she had developed for Clay.

There was no way she would be able to do that. Particularly not when it came to Clay. She'd fallen so hard in love with him that a piece of her heart would always belong to Clayton Ramos for as long as she lived.

"Gemma, you may now kiss your husband. And Tom, you may kiss your wife."

An uproarious cheer erupted from the wedding party and the steel drum band waiting in the wings began to play. Dancing commenced right away. As she hoped he would, Tori found Clay heading in her direction.

"You look beautiful," he told her when he reached her side.

She gave a playful bow. "I'm just glad this isn't a formal attire wedding. I didn't pack anything that would have suited."

His gaze assessed her from head to toe and she felt heat rush to her cheeks then travel down her entire body. "I'd say that dress suits you just fine."

Would he be taking it off her later? Something told her that was not meant to be, and a wave of sadness washed over her before she shook it off. "Thanks, you're looking pretty dapper yourself."

"The cake looks amazing. You did a fantastic job."

"This will be a first for me. I've actually never seen one of my cakes get smashed in anyone's face before."

He chuckled softly but it sounded forced. Alarm bells began ringing in her head. Something was off. Clay was back to the aloof, distant version of himself. She wasn't sure what to make of it.

He extended his hand to her. "Walk with me."

They strolled further along the beach, the music and chatter of the party growing softer and lower behind them with each step.

"Something going on?" she asked when she couldn't stand it any longer.

"I'm not sure how long the party will go— I'm guessing till the early morning hours—but I'm going to make it an early night and head to my room right after the cake is cut."

And he wasn't telling her that because he wanted to invite her to go up with him. She would be naïve to think that. Everything from Clay's body stance to the tone of his voice told her so.

"I see."

"I'll be flying back to Logan first thing after breakfast tomorrow."

Tori's breath hitched in her throat. This was really happening. He really was saying good-bye. Tori wanted the sea behind her to rise and carry her away so she didn't have to listen to any more of this. She bit down on her lip to keep if from trembling.

"I haven't even told my sisters yet. I'll let them know as soon as they stop dancing long enough."

"Why the sudden rush?"

"There's a matter I have to tend to in Boston."

"I'm sorry to hear that." She knew she was making a mistake, but the next words she uttered seemed to spill out of her mouth before she could stop them. "Maybe once I get back to Boston I'll get in touch…"

The grimace on his face told her more than any words could. She felt a shattering sensation in the vicinity of her heart.

"I won't be there for long, Tori."

She swallowed. "Why's that?"

"I've accepted an assignment in Amsterdam. I'll be there for the next year or so."

For a split second, Tori wondered if she'd heard him correctly.

"You what?"

"I've accepted a job overseas."

Where was this coming from? He'd completely blindsided her. "You didn't say anything." She was surprised her mouth worked and that she could even get the words out.

"It came about rather suddenly."

"So suddenly you didn't even think to mention it before this?"

He merely nodded. She knew then that there was nothing more to say. How naïve she'd been, how utterly clueless. That he could so easily turn away from her with such finality. As far as Clay was concerned, she'd served her purpose and he was ready to leave behind everything they'd shared together.

She'd move on from this. She'd somehow find a way to get past it. It would take time and it would hurt. But she'd dusted herself off before and built a life for herself that she could be proud of. That's what she had to focus on now. She couldn't let old doubts and insecurities come crashing back in just because she'd misread Clay so thoroughly.

She would find a way to heal.

It took everything she had to continue standing upright, to keep her knees from giving out underneath her. His rejection was complete. When she could finally get her legs to move, she turned and walked away.

CHAPTER THIRTEEN

THE CAKE WAS a big hit. As dawn approached and the last tiki torch extinguished, and the handful of revelers finally drunkenly stumbled away, the cake had proven to be one of the evening's highlights. Tori had done an outstanding job. He'd never doubted it, of course.

She'd also done an amazing job of avoiding him all night. Not that he could really blame her. He'd been pretty straightforward. But what point would there have been in delaying the inevitable?

By the time he'd walked to his room, they hadn't shared so much as a wave goodbye.

Clay snapped his travel case closed and ran through a mental checklist to ensure he had everything. He felt disoriented and out of sorts. Insomnia had plagued him when he'd tried to catch at least a couple hours of sleep. The bed felt empty. His soul felt cold. But he'd done what needed to be done.

Better for Tori to go live the rest of her life believing that he was an uncaring bastard. And the next time he needed to hire a talented baker…well, he would have to cross that proverbial bridge when it appeared.

A knock on the door snapped him alert. The car service was early.

But it wasn't a driver standing across the threshold when he opened the door.

His sisters stood there, glaring at him. Adria wore a rigid frown. Gemma, disheveled and drowsy, looked like she was ready to feed him to the wolves.

They walked past him into the room. "Come in," he said sarcastically with a flourish of his hand. Whatever was going on with them, he really didn't have time for it.

"Have a seat, big brother." Gemma pulled him over to the sofa and physically pushed him down by his shoulders. For someone with such a slight build, she was surprisingly strong.

"Can I help you two? What are you doing here?" He pointed at Gemma. "You just got married a few hours ago."

"I know. But we need to chat," Gemma began. "And considering last night was my wedding night, I have to warn you, I'm not big on patience right now."

So they weren't taking the news very well, then.

"That was quite a bombshell you dropped on us last night," Gemma charged while Adria nodded her agreement. "Didn't see that coming at all."

If they only knew.

"I apologize for that," he said, meaning it wholeheartedly. He really was sorry about the way it had all come about. But now that his decision had been made, he didn't want to dally. There was no point delaying the inevitable.

"You're just going to move across the globe?" Gemma blustered.

"For the better part of the year?" Adria added.

"I'll visit often," he reassured them. "And you can all come visit me. Lilly will get a kick out of the canals and we can take her to a tulip field."

"Somehow I think she'd prefer to have her uncle in town for her next birthday."

Clay sighed, striving for patience. "It's done, ladies. And the sooner I get back to Boston, the sooner I can wrap things up and prep for this new role." It made no sense to stick around some island in the Bahamas when he was about to start a whole new chapter of his life.

"Is that why you're leaving? So you can wrap up and prep?"

That sounded like a trick question. What choice did he have but to walk into the trap? "Why else?"

"Because it looks an awful lot like you're just simply running away."

He scoffed. "What would I be running from?"

Adria stepped around the couch, her hands on her hips. "The question is more like *who* you're running away from, I'd say."

"That's ridiculous. I'm making a career decision that feels right for this point in my life. That's all there is to it." The words sounded hollow even to his own ears. He certainly didn't seem to be convincing either one of his perturbed siblings. He felt compelled to explain further given their disbelieving expressions. "You two are both hitched now. You have your own lives. It's about time I started living mine."

"Kind of sudden, don't you think?"

"I can be impulsive like everyone else."

Adria actually laughed out loud at that. "You've never been impulsive a day in your life."

"I'm turning over a new leaf." That was a rather lame statement and the expression on both their faces told him they thought so, too.

"You're just turning over," Gemma said. "And giving up before you have a chance to fail."

He had no response. On some level, he knew her point was valid, knew that's what he'd been doing. But the underlying issues remained unchanged. "I'm no good for her. I can't be what she needs."

He couldn't even tell which one of them sucked in a breath first. "You don't mean that," Gemma told him. "You've just spent so much of your life looking over your shoulder that now you're afraid to look forward."

Adria nodded. "Take the chance, Clay. She's worth it. You know she is."

Gemma walked over and took both his hands in her small ones. "That man took away a lot of your childhood. He took away our mother. Don't let him take away your shot at happiness."

He absorbed Gemma's words as they permeated his soul. They were both right. He'd been such a fool. But what was done was done.

"Look, there's only so much I can do now. The wheels have been set in motion. I've accepted the offer and booked a flight."

"Huh. I always thought my big brother could do anything." Adria's voice dripped with mock surprise.

He ran his hand through his hair. Maybe they had a point. He at least owed Tori more of a conversation after all they'd shared together. "I'll go talk to her now. She's probably up."

"Too late," Gemma quipped with no small amount of derision.

"What? Why?"

"She's back in Boston. She took a red-eye last night. She's already gone."

"I could have done this cake in my sleep."

Tori set the simple sheet cake on the counter and grabbed a box from the cabinet below to begin packaging it. Hard to believe it had already been a week and a half since she'd returned from her fateful trip to the Bahamas. She wished she could say things were beginning to return to normal. But normal wasn't what she wanted.

The problem was, she wanted what she couldn't have.

"It's what the customer ordered," Shawna replied. "Who are we to tell him it's boring."

Boring certainly was an apt description. Single-layer marble cake with buttercream frosting. Not even a request for fruit filling. "Are you sure we took down the order right? He didn't even ask for some kind of custom-made figurine? Not even a flower?" Flowers made her think of tulips. Tulips made her think of Amsterdam. And that made her think of Clay.

Almost everything made her think of Clay. If anything, she should be thanking her lucky stars that one of her cake orders was this simple. It had been hard to concentrate on much since she'd returned.

Had he left yet? Was he even now riding a canal boat down one of Amsterdam's waterways? How easily had he moved on?

Did he even think of her?

"The client's exact words were, 'I just need a plain old cake that'll feed about twenty,'" Shawna said as she pulled a batch of homemade brownies from the oven.

"Huh. He could have gone to a grocery store for this."

Shawna shrugged. "He could have. But he wanted an authentic Tori Preston creation."

Tori rolled her eyes. "I would hardly call this a creation."

She carefully lifted the cake and placed it in the box then folded and taped up the sides. "In any case, it's ready for the delivery service."

Shawna swiveled in her direction. "Oh, bad

news on that front. They said they're not available today."

"What? That's never happened before. Did they give you any kind of explanation?"

"Some kind of emergency. Luckily that's the only order that needs to get out this afternoon."

"Well, how are we supposed to get it there?"

"Guess we have to deliver it ourselves."

"That's just great. Not like we have a bakery to run."

"Do you mind doing it, Tori? My back's been acting up and I don't think I have it in me to handle that drive sitting so long."

"Long drive? Where is it going?"

"Hyannis. Near the docks."

The Cape? She had to make her own delivery and it was all the way to the Cape.

Tori sighed, resigned to the circumstances. Maybe a long drive wouldn't be such a bad thing. It would give her some time to come to terms with all she'd have to accept about her life now that she'd had a chance to finally experience true love only to lose it within a span of mere days. It was so much worse to know exactly what you were missing out on.

"All right. Guess I'll be on my way."

She could have sworn she heard Shawna giggle as she walked out the kitchen door.

* * *

An hour and a half later, Tori parked and pulled her delivery out of the specialty cooler, rechecking the address. Something wasn't quite right. When Shawna had said the docks, Tori had assumed the destination would be one of the houses across the water or a restaurant or café near the port authority.

But the number didn't match any of the buildings. Could it be a dock number? Was this cake supposed to go on a boat?

Strange detail to leave out of the delivery instructions.

She had taken several steps, studying slip numbers, when it came into view. The *Ocean Nomad*. A children's cruise boat. Or more accurately, a modern-day replica pirate ship.

Her pulse pounded through her veins as a strange kind of hope blossomed in her chest.

Clay leaned over the railing of the replica frigate and watched as Tori approached. For several moments, he simply allowed himself to take in the sight of her.

A physical ache tugged at his heart. He'd missed her.

The days spent without her had been miserable and lonely. He'd been a fool to think he'd be able to spend his life without her in it. He'd barely survived less than two weeks apart. Even before Gemma and Adria had barreled into his room that morning, his regret had started to ignite like the beginning spark of a wildfire.

He couldn't let the past rob him of his opportunity for a bright and love-filled future. It was high time he told all that to Tori.

The look of confusion on her face just made her look all the more fetching. She held the cake box precariously as she glanced around, trying to determine where to go.

Clay's pulse beat hard through his veins, his muscles taut. It shocked him to realize he was nervous.

What if it all goes wrong? What if she isn't ready to forgive me?

It would no doubt serve him right. He'd been a downright bastard to her the night of the wedding. All because she'd exposed a vulnerability in him he hadn't wanted to acknowledge.

So he'd pushed her away and might very well have lost the one woman who could serve as a light for the darkness he'd lived through.

Hopefully, he wouldn't be wearing that cake she carried by the time this was over.

Only one way to find out. Uttering a silent prayer, he cupped his hands around his lips and called out to her.

* * *

A hauntingly familiar voice sounded through the air.

"Ahoy there, matey."

Tori turned so fast on her heel she almost dropped the cake box.

Standing on the deck, beneath a black-and-white skull and crossbones flag, was Clay.

She knew she wasn't imagining things. It was really him. Flesh and blood, and wearing a silly pirate's hat. The one she'd left behind at the resort in her haste to leave. The toy cutlass hung loosely in his belt.

The mystery of it all slowly began to unravel. Shawna had to have been in on it, which explained the giggle Tori had heard on her way out.

Her jaw agape, Tori could only watch as Clay lowered the wooden ramp and walked down to where she stood frozen in shock.

"Clay?"

"Hey, sweetheart."

"Hey, yourself." Again with the witty conversation, just like back in the Bahamas by the pool. She had to cut herself some slack, though. She was lucky she could find any words at all.

He chuckled, wandering closer until she could see the golden specks of his eyes. He sported a smattering of dark stubble, adding an authenticity to the pirate getup. It was all so ridiculous and fantastic and hard to believe. She'd missed him so much, her body ached with the urge to touch him. But she seemed unable to move a muscle.

"I thought you were in Amsterdam."

"Couldn't bring myself to go."

"You couldn't?"

He shook his head. "No. Not worth what I might be leaving behind. My life is here. My family's here. By the way, did you know I'll be getting another little niece or nephew soon?"

She had to come clean on that score. "I actually did know that."

He smiled that handsome smile of his, the one that made her insides go squishy. The smile she hadn't been able to get out of her mind when she lay awake at night missing him with every fiber of her being.

"I kind of figured you might have," he said, tapping her nose playfully. "And then there's the most important thing I didn't want to leave behind."

"What's that?"

"The woman I love."

"Oh, Clay."

"I behaved mutinously. Please forgive me."

It was so very tempting to simply throw herself into his arms. Her body ached to be held in his embrace, she longed to thrust her fingers through his hair and to pull his face to hers for a deep and lingering kiss. But she couldn't make it that easy on him. He owed her more than that. He'd delivered quite a blow to her heart and to her spirit when he'd walked away from her so easily.

"It's not that simple..." she began. "I'm afraid I might need some convincing. How do I know you won't be tempted by another job offer at some point?"

He shook his head slowly. "I'm not going anywhere unless you agree to come with me. You have my word."

She sucked in a breath. She believed him; sincerity rang true and clear in his voice. "I have half a mind to throw this at you, you know." With one hand, she raised the box that held the cake.

He chuckled and took hold of her free hand. "I figured as much. It's why I ordered such a plain one."

She resisted the urge to laugh. "You're going to have to make it up to me somehow, Clay. The way you tried to run off before you came to your senses..."

He lifted her chin, his gaze focused fully on

her face. "I know, sweetheart. I vow to do just that. As long as it takes."

Tori felt her already flimsy resolve slowly start to drain away. How was she supposed to stand firm when he looked at her like that?

Maybe she was weak, but she wanted him too much to pretend anymore. She longed for him to hold her, to kiss her. She needed his touch as much as her next breath.

"Okay," she said with a sniffle.

"You have every right to tell me to go walk the plank. But I'm asking instead if you'll walk to me down the aisle." Before she could process exactly what was happening, he pulled out a small velvet box.

"Victoria Preston, will you do me the honor of marrying me?"

The cake didn't stand a chance. It slipped right out of her hand as she threw her arms around him.

"Yes!" she called out with all the jubilation and joy flooding through her heart. "I would follow you across the seas, my love."

EPILOGUE

VILARDO'S TRATTORIA WAS closed for the evening, a rare occurrence for a Saturday during the height of summer. There was a good and happy reason for the closure, though—a private event that just happened to be the wedding ceremony of the proprietors' only daughter.

It wasn't a large gathering by many standards. But everyone Tori loved and cared about was in attendance. Most of them currently on the dance floor. Including Clay, who had Lilly on his shoulders as he danced across from Tori's mom. The man apparently had impressive balancing skills. Rhythm? Not so much. Tori would have be sure to tease him about that later when they were finally alone.

"I told you the dress was lucky."

Tori tore her gaze away from the man she loved—who, as of three hours ago, now happened to be her husband—at the sound of her sister's voice.

Eloise had helped her with every detail of her wedding day. Tori didn't know what she would have done without her.

"I think you're the actual good luck charm," she told her twin, running her hand over the silky material. Eloise had gifted Tori the dress after her own wedding, with instructions to go after the man of her dreams. "The dress is just an added bonus."

Eloise didn't get a chance to answer. Her husband swooped up behind her and spun her around with a mischievous grin until she started dancing with him. Josh had gotten even more playful since becoming a husband. He and Eloise were made for each other.

Just as Clay was made for her.

Tori watched as he gently set his niece down and bowed to her mother before turning away. Their eyes met over the crowd of dancers and the love that shone in his nearly knocked the breath out of her. How had she gotten so fortunate?

He approached her now from across the dance floor doing a silly version of the electric slide. Taking her by the waist, he dipped her and wiggled his eyebrows.

"Dance with me," he said with a laugh as he brought her back to him.

She answered by pressing herself against his

length and swaying slowly to the music despite the fast tempo of the song.

"I love the way you dance," he whispered in her ear.

"Even to kiddie reggae?" she asked.

He chuckled at the reminder of the time they'd "danced" together by the pool all those weeks ago in the Bahamas. "As long as you're in my arms."

Tears of joy filled her eyes. Everyone around them may as well have disappeared. Even the sound of the loud music seemed to dull in her ears. Her focus narrowed completely on the man she'd be spending the rest of her life with.

"There's nowhere else I'd rather be."

* * * * *

*If you missed the previous story in the
How to Make a Wedding duet,
then check out*

From Bridal Designer to Bride
by Kandy Shepherd

*And if you enjoyed this story,
check out these other great reads from
Nina Singh*

**Her Inconvenient Christmas Reunion
Spanish Tycoon's Convenient Bride
Her Billionaire Protector**

All available now!